THE ALIEN'S SECRET

Don Sealey

The Alien's Secret
Copyright ©2024 Don Sealey

ISBN 978-1506-914-83-1 PBK
ISBN 978-1506-914-84-8 EBK

LCCN 2024927633

December 2024

Published and Distributed by
First Edition Design Publishing, Inc.
P.O. Box 17646, Sarasota, FL 34276-3217
www.firsteditiondesignpublishing.com

I dedicate this story to my wife, my family, my friends, and my faith. Family and friends please know that I will be forever blessed by your friendship, love, and support. They mean more to me than you could possibly imagine.

As to my faith,

This book is an expression of my belief about the Power of God which informs us of the correct way to behave toward others. For example, when a cashier gives us more change than the transaction requires, what do we do? Unless we were raised by wolves, we all know which choice is the right choice. Either we return it (good behavior) or we keep it and slink away, knowing what we did was wrong. Knowing the right thing to do is inspired, I believe, by the Power of God.

Finally, I like to recall the quote by Russell Crow in the movie, Gladiator. He said, "What we do in life echoes in eternity." Take that as you like, but those of us who try to live according to God's Law can sleep a lot more soundly on our last night on Earth than those who have disregarded it. By that time, the time to choose sides will probably have passed.

From the Author

This writing is not a scientifically researched piece of academic analysis. It is a piece of fiction based on known facts which have a basis in science. For example, there will be reference to the universe. The universe is, in fact, so large and the edges of the universe are so far away that current science is unable to accurately measure the size of the universe. If current estimates, however inaccurate they may be, are helpful to you then the current judgement of the size of the universe is 92-94 billion light years from one side to another. If you think about something that size, it is quite amazing.

The universe is comprised of galaxies which are groupings of stars and planets. To date the estimate of the number of galaxies in the observable universe ranges from 100 billion galaxies to over 2 trillion galaxies. The uncertainty in the number of galaxies is because we cannot currently see the edge of the universe so an exact tally is impossible.

I would be remiss if I failed to mention the name of the galaxy of which we are a part. Earth belongs to the Milky Way galaxy which can sometime be seen on a clear night. The Milky Way is about 13.6 billion years old and contains an estimated 100- 400 billion stars. Our sun is one of those stars. The sun, the earth, and our sister planets form our solar system.

If these numbers are not enough to boggle your mind, let me take you one step farther. In the universe, not all stars or planets came into existence at the same time. Stars are basically collections of hot gasses, mostly hydrogen and helium, and each star has its own life cycle ranging from a few million years to trillions of years. Scientists estimate that our own galaxy produces from 10 to 20 new stars each year.

At end of a star's life, the star runs out of gaseous material to keep the star alive and it begins to expand. The expansion of the star will produce the effect of drawing the star closer to nearby planets in its solar system causing an increase in temperatures for the unfortunate planets closest to the dying star.

Science estimates that our own sun will come to an end of its fuel supply and will begin the slow crawl to the end of its existence in several billion years. This important estimate forms the basis of the push by NASA and others to colonize new worlds before ours becomes uninhabitable. Not to worry, our sun still has several billion more years to go.

When a civilization attains a certain level of technological sophistication, its attention inevitably turns to space exploration. There are several incentives to divert resources to space exploration. However, among the most pressing is the one mentioned above.

Delivery systems are designed to propel beings and equipment into space. The initial excitement of blasting people and equipment into space quickly faces the hard reality that about 90% of a rocket's weight is relegated to propellant required to overcome the pull of gravity. Gravity limits the payloads of other things that can be lifted into space.

The space elevator is currently in the conceptual design phase but its purpose is to replace the need for rockets which require literally tons of fuel. The space elevator is vastly cheaper than the traditional chemically boosted propulsion systems and can be used repeatedly to carry beings and equipment into space where they can be transferred to waiting space exploration vehicles.

This promising addition to the field of space exploration consists of four basic components. First is the base station which is attached to the planet's surface located near the planet's equator. Next is a tether which stretches from the ground into space. The length of the tether varies but initially will be about 23,000 miles long with conceptual plans for a tether stretching over 60,000 miles. The tether is the only part of the four basic components of the space elevator that is still in the developmental design phase. At the other end of the tether will be a counterweight located in a geosynchronous orbit above the planet's surface. The most probable configuration for the counterweight will be a permanent space station.

The counterweight can be thought of as a ball on the end of a string. When the ball is spun around in a circular motion, or orbit, the ball stays taut at the end of the string. If the ball comes loose from the string, the string will fall. If the ball does not spin fast enough, the ball and the string will fall. This is exactly the concept of the space elevator. The only addition is that the ball, or counterweight, is a space docking station which can house people and equipment as they prepare to launch into space.

The fourth element of the space elevator is the elevator car or gantry which will lift people and equipment up the tether to the waiting space station. From the space station, people and equipment can be transferred from the gantry into waiting space ships for deployment into space.

Names and Places for reference:

Valerion - Ruler of Elon
Seth Walker - Leader of the rebellion
Megan - Walker's ex-wife. She had recently worked for Valerion
Max Walker - Seth Walker's brother
JP - Seth Walker's best friend
Conrad Pincus - Works for Valerion as an assassin
Naroobian system - Home planetary system of The Builders
Anya - An ET and one of The Builders
Yardak - A band of space pirates
Sorrengia - A planet that may be a home for Valerion's space armada
Elon - Home planet for Walker and Valerion
Lordune – a planet in the Naroobian system which will be the home of The People.

CHAPTER 1

The sole ruler of the dying planet, Elon, who was euphemistically called "President" Valerion, glared through the tempered glass window scanning the surface like a starving vulture looking for prey. Yet, from his presidential fortress, all that could be seen was the burnt orange wasteland, which was the residue of his world. Centuries ago, Elon was a lush planet rich in forests, rivers, lakes, and oceans, but now was a smoldering ball of rock. Today, outside the window, everything organic has been reduced to ash by the fierce heat of Elon's dying sun. Elon's sun was closing in on the hapless planet because the sun grew larger as the it reached the final stage of its life cycle.

His chief of internal security, Kord, stood behind him deferentially. He could see Valerion's hawk-like face reflected in the glass and almost feel the rage burning inside him. Valerion's foremost obsession was to destroy the rebels, "vermin" as he liked to call them, so his domination of every living soul on Elon would be complete.

On the other hand, Kord's primary concern was getting off Elon alive. This concern far outweighed any thoughts of the well-being of a few thousand rebels.

Valerion's bony jaw tightened when he muttered through clenched teeth, "They mock me every day they live." The fact that they were still alive made his blood boil.

"Yes Excellency," Kord whispered, bowing his head in deference.

The bane of Valerion's existence, Seth Walker, must be eliminated. Walker was the rebel leader. Walker first encountered Valerion years earlier at Space Academy when they were both students competing for top honors at the prestigious science institute.

The final insult to Valerion, handed to him by Walker, occurred when his only daughter fled the royal palace to join the rebels. She became increasingly repelled by her father's murderous methods of controlling the opposition. She sought to assuage her conscience by joining the rebels.

Her unannounced departure was a source of persistent embarrassment to Valerion. His official explanation for her absence was that she was killed by the resistance, but Kord knew different. He knew the truth.

Valerion pounded a boney fist against the window expressing his rage. The population of Elon had shrunk for hundreds of years while competing political factions battled for ultimate control of what remained of the people of the planet. Rising heat over the centuries has taken its toll on vegetation, livestock, and millions of starved. Now, only the friends of Valerion's movement, the elite one-percenters, had access to climate-controlled agro-complexes where food could be grown away from heat, a process developed by Walker. These large mini-farms are known as biopods.

Kord spoke, trying to ease Valerion from his fit of rage, "Excellency," he paused gathering his nerve, "may I propose that we bring the transport ships down to the surface and load as many people as we can onto them and get away from this planet? When we are a safe distance away from our decaying sun, we can send expendable soldiers down the space elevators as hunter/seeker units to locate the rebels and dispose of them."

"Everyone is well aware that we need to leave," Valerion said blithely without turning to provide the courtesy of a face-to-face response.

"Yes, Excellency," Kord nodded.

"Of course you are right," said Valerion, almost as an afterthought. "We need to get off this smoldering rock before it is consumed by our dying sun. But I absolutely despise leaving while I have a chance to destroy Walker personally and exact revenge for my daughter's death at the hands of the resistance."

"I understand," said Kord who was one of the very few who knew the embarrassing truth about Valerion's daughter's defection to the rebel cause.

In an unaccustomed moment of introspection, Valerion uttered, "I almost got rid of Walker several months ago but the explosive devise meant for him took out his wife and General Woodley instead. Without their leader, the rebel horde would be the most vulnerable. Unfortunately. It appears that all I did was piss off Walker and strengthened the rebels' will to survive. Unfortunately, it unified them against me."

"Excellency, there will be widespread panic when the transports arrive. Who do we allow to come with us into space and who will be left behind to certain death?"

"For the most part, we will take our closest allies, or, should I say, our most compliant followers. I have purged all the independent thinkers on the planet except for Walker and his group of deplorables." Valerion moved away from the window and the heat from outside. "In addition, we will take one transport filled with workers, slaves if you will. We will need them when we find and settle on the next planet. One, just one, transport for them for the duration of the voyage."

"How will I know who to allow on board the transports?"

"I will tell you."

CHAPTER 2

Several hours after Valerion and his armada of space transports loaded up and left Elon, Walker strained to open the heavy blast door of the rebels' mountain stronghold and step outside into the searing heat with his friend Jack Powers, or JP as he was called.

JP had worked his way into Walker's inner circle by being, as Walker liked to say, "really good at blowing things up." But for Walker, it was more than JP's pyrotechnic skills. JP was a friend on whom Walker could always rely to have his back. In Walker's world, this kind of loyalty was a precious commodity that kept him alive many times.

Both men squinted to protect their eyes from the heat and debris howling across the lifeless terrain. Walker needed a short reprieve from the palpable sense of anxiety among The People inside the fortress. The People grew more restless each day while preparing to leave the only home they had ever known and journey into space to search for a new home planet.

Walker turned to his friend and reminisced about Valerion's leaving, "You know, it would have been easier if they used the space elevators to get off the planet but it almost seemed like he wanted to make a production for The People saying 'see, now we are gone and you are not.'"

JP responded, "That may be true, but I am glad we are landing space cruisers and loading The People and getting out of here quickly. I have no interest in crawling up the gantry for hours. Too many things can go wrong."

"You are right. No more talk about that. We have our plan set and we will stick to the plan." Walker replied.

Walker was the only person to defy Valerion and live. That act of defiance was essentially the beginning of the rebellion. Although he would only share this with JP, Walker knew that the odds of getting The People off their home planet were stacked against them.

The People's anxiety level reached a fever pitch when they saw Valerion's space armada load up and lift off the planet surface. Walker promised that it would be their turn to leave in just 24 hours. The People were physically and emotionally ready to go.

Walker and Powers closed the heavy blast door and ducked behind a fifteen-foot-high boulder. A caustic sulfur stench caused by gas vapors released from below the surface forced both men to reach their gas masks.

Before he could put on his mask, Walker bent over to extract a grain of wind-blown dirt from his eye when a bright blue electric pulse from a sniper rifle nearly missed his ear and shattered the top half of the boulder. Both men had to cover their heads from the showers of rock fragments falling on them. They sought refuge behind what remained of the boulder and Walker spoke calmly into his radio, "Colonel Morgan, I believe we just located the last shooter you were chasing. He just took a shot at JP and me in front of blast door number four."

JP reached for his sidearm saying, "That was too close. I am not waiting for Morgan to find the shooter. I'll go deal with that one. Who knows, he might be shooting at me next time."

They exchanged wide-eyed glances when another burst of automatic pulse fire filled the air. Colonel Morgan radioed the General, "I wish that was the last one, sir, but now we need to deal with the latest group of insurgents sent here by Valerion."

"Colonel, you can bet Valerion will keep sending down hit squads as long as we keep staying alive."

"They will keep coming until we get off this rock," JP said raising his voice in frustration.

"Gentlemen," said Walker, "here is the situation. Obviously, we must leave this planet and there are only two ways to do that. Both ways require the use of transports. Either the transports pick us up from the elevator docking stations 22,000 miles above Elon or they pick us up from the surface of Elon like Valerion's pilots did for his people two days ago. Many of the best pilots in Space Command have joined the Rebellion and they are just waiting for our signal to come and get us."

"I am absolutely certain it is driving Valerion berserk wondering where we have our transports hidden," said Walker not able to hold back a satisfied grin.

"If I was Valerion and if I was thinking clearly, I would send enough troops to Elon to prevent us from leaving the planet and just let us burn to death. The major drawback of this strategy is that he has a recruiting problem in that not many troops up there want to return to Elon and take a chance to burn to death along with us. Not only that, but every hour his troops stay here trying to kill us, Valerion's armada flies away as fast as they can leave the hit squads return to Valerion's armada highly in doubt. However, the aspect of this situation most in our favor is that Valerion is not thinking clearly."

A hand clapped Walker on the shoulder, sending a jolt of adrenaline through the general's core.

Reaching for his side arm, he spun. His mouth curved into a smile when he saw his brother, Max, smiling at him. "Good God, little brother, sneaking up on a person like that can get your head blown off." He holstered his weapon.

"We had better get back inside before we all melt or die from the fumes" said Max who was putting on his own gas mask. "We may be the last people on this planet and all of us will have a better chance of leaving here if we stay out of the way of sniper fire and help put our evacuation plan into effect."

Big brother Walker said," in about six hours we will lead The People to the space transports which will land at pre-determined locations and get off this smoking rock while we still can. For sure, no one will be getting much sleep tonight. However, I need you to make certain that everyone is with their group and that each group knows which elevator to use. Finally," said Walker almost yelling above the whirling winds, "it is critical that you be in contact with the transport pilots who will be picking us up at our assigned stations."

"God's speed, my friends."

CHAPTER 3

Returning to the relative comfort of the reinforced bunker with its polished floors and shiny metal walls and away from the smell of burning organic matter, Max said, "Valerion appears to have plenty of expendable soldiers. They know where we are and as soon as we start to leave Elon, we will be sitting ducks."

"That is why Morgan and his group are constantly searching for insurgents. Last night he located another large cell of them at the base of the space elevator near the lake in the valley," said Seth. "There really is no idea how many hit teams are here or might be coming."

"So, again, we are being hunted by Valerion," said Max, his exasperation showing.

"Yes, but this time it feels different," said the younger Walker. "The last of Valerion's attack force arrived twenty-four hours ago. They are heavily armed, but do not show the will to leave the safety of being close to their space elevator. That space elevator is their only lifeline back to the safety of space."

"What do you think makes this group timider than the others?"

"Elon is clearly down to its last few hours of being habitable. I guess Valerion's troops do not want to get too far from their space elevator and get into a protracted fight. I ordered Morgan's units to deal with tonight. I am going to tag along with Morgan because I cannot sleep with all this excitement. Also, we cannot afford to run into any surprises," said the General.

A look of concern flashed over Max's face as the older brother who he idolized hinted that he was going out on a high-risk patrol. "Why you, Seth? Why not send out some of the younger soldiers? You are the only one who knows all the pieces of the plan for us to leave tomorrow."

Seth puts his hand on Max's shoulder. "Listening, little brother, the plan for us to leave has been in place for some time. All we must do is get our people to the space elevators as soon as we get the all-clear from Morgan that he has neutralized Valerion's group of assassins. Beside that, what kind of a man would I be if I gave this assignment to someone else because I out-ranked him or her?"

Li Kang, one of the senior section leaders, caught Walker's attention.

"We have a lot of uneasy people waiting for the all-clear signal to leave," she said. "You two have been at the forefront of the struggle for a long time and it would be helpful if you could make an effort to reassure them."

Walker smiled and winked at Li, one of the rebellions' most trusted officers. Interestingly, Li was Valerion's daughter, who fled her father's barbarous methods of dealing with his adversaries. She found a rewarding life with the rebellion several years ago. For obvious reasons, she changed her name from Margaret Ann Valerion to Li Kang to conceal her identity.

Walker said, "Go, Max, and reassure The People."

"I know they would like to see you too, General," said Max.

"Not now. I have an important task to take care of with Colonel Morgan."

Li could not hold her tongue any longer. She said, "General, with all due respect, Colonel Morgan and his band of crazies enjoy living in the danger zone and are often outside our defensive perimeter looking for fights with enemy soldiers. You are not going..."

"Li," the General interrupted her, "I must do what I believe is best for The People. That's all that really matters."

After turning her back on her father, Li had a strong feeling of allegiance to Walker, who she thought of as a big brother. "Please let me go with you to watch your back," she pleaded.

"Li," as he turned to face her, he said with a toothy grin, "you need to go with Max. If I let you come with me then I will have to let Max come and who knows how many others." He said, "Your job is to take care of The People and help them get off this planet. They must survive and find a new home in the universe where people like them can flourish. They are the last of Elon's freedom seekers with a stubborn will to resist Valerion's lust to dominate everyone under his control."

"I understand, sir," she said as she hung her head with the look of someone who just lost an argument with one of their parents.

Max put his arm around Li's shoulder and pulled her away, "Come on, Li. Let's go do some hand holding and let the General do his job."

As they walked, Li faked a smile. "I don't have a great feeling about this."

A few steps later, Max said, "I wish I could disagree."

CHAPTER 4

Seth knows that Ed Morgan is an excellent soldier. He proven himself to be a leader in battle when he was under the command of Walker's lifelong friend TJ Woodley. Unfortunately, five months ago Woodley and Seth Walker's wife were killed in an assassination attempt intended for Seth. Now he had no choice but to put Morgan in command of this mission which would have life or death consequences for The People.

"Ed," said Walker over a comm link, "why don't you bring your team inside the bunker so we can go over the plan one more time and they can get some food and some well-earned rest."

As Morgan's team came inside the mountain stronghold, Walker said, "Nice work on that sniper, Ed. He was better than most," Walker said rubbing the ear that the sniper almost shot off."

The two senior military leaders walked slowly through the gleaming, cylindrical halls of the underground bunker discussing the details of the operation that was about to take place only eight miles away.

As they walked, Morgan, who was new to Walker's inner circle of confidants, asked, "Why is Valerion so obsessed with our destruction?"

"That's a reasonable question, Ed. I asked myself that more than once. I believe he hates us because we are the only ones on the planet too stubborn to conquer. It is either that or he just hates me and is taking it out on The People."

Morgan looked at Walker with a sly smile,' Why would he hate you more than the rest of us? You don't seem too overly dislikable."

Walker stopped and leaned against several boxes of rifles. He thought back to the struggles between Valerion and himself which began decades ago at Space Academy. Sadly, it was probably that competition that cost his wife her life when Valerion tried to have him killed.

"We were classmates at the Space Academy. The two of us were in a four-year struggle to become the number one in the class. But during our senior year, Valerion designed a science experiment for his senior class project concerning how long it would take for Elon to become too hot to sustain life in that our sun was not only dying but expanding in size at the same time."

"Unfortunately for him, I proved that Valerion had plagiarized his science work and, as a result, he was expelled from the academy and forced to repeat his senior year. He would have done anything to graduate at the top of his class, but in his twisted mind he felt that I took all that away from him. After that humiliation, he hated me and everyone else with a passion. Since that time, he has been trying to prove that he was better than everyone and set out on a mission to control the entire world."

"Even before Space Academy, the young Valerion was obsessed with power and control. His father was a minor bureaucrat in the capital and was continually frustrated by being passed over for promotions by others who he felt were less deserving. His father's self-loathing cast him into a pit of depression, which resulted in the abuse of his son and wife. Ultimately, his father killed himself."

"That kind of childhood has to warp a person," said Morgan.

"After his father died, the young Valerion was embittered and changed forever. Whatever it took, he was determined to acquire power by any means necessary and use it to advance his own personal agenda which was to wield control over others."

"Enough of this memory lane stuff," Walker huffed, wanting to move on to more important matters. "Let's go over the plan one more time."

"Whatever you say, sir," Morgan responded. "After you and JP land on the platform, we begin the bombardment of the reinforced compound where they are sheltered. After four minutes of shock and awe bombardment, I open a communication link with their commander and present their options to them. I will convince them to surrender and flee the planet by way of the space elevator or, if they refuse, we will cut the elevator cable and the troops will be faced with certain death because their only method of returning to space will have been destroyed."

The two military leaders searched each other's face for any suggestion that there could be a more humane set of choices for these troops than burning to death or returning to Valerion who has a very low tolerance for failure.

"I don't mean to get off topic, sir, but do I need to remind you that this group of assassins is under the command of Conrad Pincus. He used to be one of ours who betrayed The People and tried to assassinate you but killed your wife and TJ instead."

Walker tuned Morgan's comments out. He thought,' I know, I know, I know. Pincus planted the bomb that was intended for me but killed my wife and your boss instead." Walker stared at the floor. His wife died five months ago. Sleep eluded him most nights. Each time when he finally fell asleep, he relived the nightmare of her death and he could not elude the feeling of survivor guilt that tortured him for having survived the blast when his two closest friends were blown apart.

He caught Morgan gazing at him. "I still think about her every day. However, I cannot afford to spend time dwelling on revenge. My job is to get The People to a new home."

Morgan grunted with affirmative sounds.

"Let's gather up your men and head back outside to the flight operations area," said Walker. There are less than six hours before we need to move The People to the landing sites for the space transports. We have a lot of work to do before then."

Morgan ordered his troops into one of the small transports. While Walker watched them board the shuttle, he stroked his chin and thought to himself with a forced smile, "But I wouldn't lose any sleep if Pincus suffered an unfortunate but deadly accident during the bombardment."

The lights of Morgan's shuttle faded into the howling darkness before Walker and JP boarded their smaller shuttle. They headed forward the landing platform at the base of the space elevator. This platform, similar to hundreds on the surface of the planet, serves as an anchor that secures the tether (a model of ingenuity and metallurgical innovation about 150 years ago) to the planet's surface. At the other end of the 22,000-mile tether was the space station.

When Morgan's group was in place, Walker gave the order. "We have landed on the platform. As soon as you commence bombardment, we will enter the control center of the platform. Commence firing."

"Cover your ears, General."

CHAPTER 5

Pincus and his troops had been back on their home planet for less than 24 hours, but apparently their appetite for engaging the resistance was low and sinking fast. They were camped at the base of a space elevator in a hardened metal building. The troops all knew the weather outside was nearing lethal level, and the winds howled like a band of banshees. In almost every respect, Elon was as close to hell as possible. If it got any worse, they would all die.

Despite being sent to wipe out The People, Pincus' personal goal was simply to avert a mutiny by his own soldiers, which would, no doubt, be very bad for him. His hit team knew that every minute spent on Elon was a minute that the space convoy, carrying every person they had ever known, sped farther away from them in search of a new home.

JP and Walker listened intently to the communication link with Morgan but there was no update. Nothing but silence. JP said to the General, "Any time now we may be visited by about sixty really pissed off enemy troops who see you and me as the only thing standing between them and getting home to Valerion's space armada."

Walker called Morgan and said, "Tell Pincus that we want all of them to surrender or we will blow the cable and they will be stuck here to burn to death with us."

Pincus responded quickly to Morgan, "I'll think about it," was his response. However, in his devious mind, he envisioned sending his troops into the howling night air to storm the control room and eliminate whoever was there. After that, they would all return to the safety of their waiting space cruiser.

After Morgan told Walker the response he got from Pincus, Walker said to Morgan, "Make sure Pincus knows that I am the one with my finger on the detonator that will blow up the tether and leave them stranded on Elon."

"I will get that message to him right away, General."

"Ed, while Pincus is mulling your last transmission, I want you to broadcast a separate message to his troops. Tell them exactly who has his finger on the button and that I want revenge for killing my wife. If they hand over Pincus alive, we will allow them to leave for the space convoy."

"On it, General."

Seconds later, a female voice addressed Morgan on the comm system. The woman described herself as second-in-command under Pincus. "Colonel Morgan, I agree to your terms. I have taken Pincus prisoner and in one minute I will send Pincus through the door into the courtyard in chains. Believe me, not one of us wanted this fight. We were forced to come back to Elon by Valerion."

"Colonel Morgan, one more favor, if I might be so bold. Please let me meet personally with you and General Walker. Given your dire situation on Elon, I have a proposal that I believe you will find well worth your time."

Morgan said to Walker, "General, Pincus' second in command has asked to speak to you on a matter of some urgency. If I may, I will escort her to meet you at the control center."

"Make it fast, Ed. We do not have a lot of time to spare. The People start to move to the landing sites for their pre-assigned space transport in about four hours and I'd like to be there with them."

From his vantage point in the control room, Walker looked down on the walkway. Morgan escorted a woman up the stairway to the control center. Something uncomfortably familiar about her silhouette and her gate unnerved Walker. Still, he wanted to know what could she want that was more urgent than getting herself and her troops up the space elevator."

"You! Well, well. Look who's here," said Walker shaking his head in disbelief. "It's my back-stabbing, ex-wife, Megan Murray. Ed, it seems the good news just keeps on getting better. Our home is about to be consumed by the sun and soldiers are being sent daily to kill us. Now, along comes my ex-wife with the deal of the century," he said with his arms outstretched and his head looking toward Heaven.

Despite his snide comments, mostly for his first wife's benefit, seeing her was a shock. It was not entirely unpleasant, but at the same time, he was still grieving for his second wife, who had been murdered by mistake just a few months earlier by Megan's employer, Valerion, his arch enemy.

"What do you have for us now, Megan?" said Walker waving his hands in frustration. "We all have important things to do."

"General, please let me tell you how sorry I was to hear of your wife's death," Megan said. "Not that you need my assurances but you have the right person in custody for the attempted assassination attack that killed her. It was Pincus who planned and carried out the attack to gain favor with Valerion. It did not work for him. Valerion was livid with Pincus for his failure to kill you. He does not tolerate failure. Therefore, while this mission to Elon was not expressly a suicide mission, if none of us ever returned from this attack, Valerion could care less."

"For once, Valerion and I agree. Why should I care, Megan?"

"As you know, Valerion is scouring this sector of the universe for a planet to occupy for his new empire. I imagine you will be doing the same thing too if you are able to escape this death trap of a planet." Megan paused and looked closely at Walker to see if he was listening. Seeing no reaction, she continued.

"One of those unfortunate souls in the brig of one of Valerion's transports, the place where Valerion stores the expendable people, is a woman whose ship crashed on Elon several years ago."

"An ET?" asked Walker, now paying attention.

"Oh, yes."

"And again, what does that do for us?' asked Walker to try to connect all the dots.

"I believe this woman knows how to return to the galaxy she came from. That Galaxy contains at least two planets that are compatible with the environmental conditions on Elon before it began to deteriorate. Instead of roaming the far reaches of the universe like pathetic gypsies, how about setting a course for a planet ready to move into?"

The gears in Walker's brain were turning as he tried to make sense of the scenario that his ex-wife was laying out for him. "Why are you telling me about this one in a trillion opportunity and why would Valerion let her help us? For that matter, what stroke of good fortune makes you willing to help us?"

"As far as Valerion is concerned, let me assure you that he does not know she exists. If he had the slightest idea that she was in the brig in one of his transports, he would already be torturing the information out of her. I also believe she would die before giving up the destination to someone like him."

"What's in it for you," demanded Walker, crossing his arms and trying to appear as disinterested as possible. Even though, this time Megan held his undivided attention.

"I know you are the perfect man, Seth" she smiled sarcastically, "and you probably have never made a mistake. Well, believe me, I have made a lot of mistakes and they haunt me every day of my life."

Walker chuckled. Just like Megan to shower him with compliments when she wanted something. However, what was her endgame here?

"I desperately want to make amends for helping Valerion cast his sick web of domination over most of the planet," she said.

Walker looked at Morgan, Megan, and then back to Morgan. "Can you think of a way we can corroborate my ex-wire's story about the ET?"

After a few seconds, which seemed like hours, passed, a voice in the back of the room said, "I can." All eyes turned toward JP. "Before I started working full time for you, General, I was assigned to the experimental prototype division of Research and Development which included detaining two ETs. I'll bet one of them is the individual Megan is talking about."

Of course, JP would know this. He was Walker's go-to man on matters such as strange and unusual happenings in Research and Development (R&D).

"Megan," Walker said, "describe the being you are talking about to JP so he can determine if his ET and yours are one in the same."

Megan thought for a moment. She looked at Walker, Morgan, and JP before answering this question. "The young lady or ET I am speaking of is named Anya. Her skin is olive green and she is from the planet named Naroobia. They are deeply religious people with a missionary zeal to spread the word of God"

JP added, "I know this story better than most. When she crashed on Elon, her spacecraft was damaged beyond repair, so she became a permanent resident of our planet. You can imagine that when a spaceship from another world crashes on our world, the government becomes extremely anxious to discover as much as it could about the matter. The fact that the crew of the ship was all green individuals made it more interesting. As the world was amid enormous turmoil due to the heat, Valerion arresting thousands of people who opposed his restriction of people's rights to speak and to assemble, as well as the continuing battles between the rebels and the government, it was decided to simply hide the remains of the space ship and imprison the two living crew members until there was time to research the matter more fully."

Walker said, "If Anya and her other crew members were so technically advanced, how could they allow their ship to crash on our planet?"

JP recounted, "Anya told me that the Naroobians were being chased by several space pirate ships who wanted their speedy space cruiser. The Naroobians were faster than the pirates, but the pirates got off a series of good cannon shots that crippled their ship. When Anya and her crew were about to crash into Elon, the pirates broke off the chase. After Anya and her crew crashed, they were taken prisoner and ultimately forgotten by Valerion's government who had more pressing matters to address such as their own survival."

"As a frequent visitor, I got to know her quite well when she was being detained in my section. After a while, when priorities were shifting as Elon was undergoing political consolidation, someone left her cell door open and she vanished into the night. Not many days later, she was recaptured by Valerion's guards and put on a space freighter. Later, she found herself in the space armada, which is where she is today.

. Walker furrowed his brow. "Tell me about her escape. You don't know anything about this escape, do you, JP?"

"Are you asking if I aided in her escape? I can't imagine doing anything like that, boss. It was just a tragic oversight," JP said, holding back a knowing smile.

"Alright," said Walker checking the time. "We need to get down to business. Because you have given this more thought than the rest of us, Megan, what do you suggest that we do with this bit of information? And before you speak, be aware that I am going to assume that whatever you say is more than likely a lie, and that you are conjuring up a trap for whoever accompanies you. That being said, do please go ahead."

"Given our past, I would expect nothing less than skepticism."

"Get on with it," he said impatiently.

"The gist of my plan involves my returning to Valerion's armada with my troops minus Pincus. When we reach the armada, the troops will return to their units. In the event they are questioned, all they will know is what they have seen: that Pincus was handed over as a prisoner to General Walker and the resistance in exchange for their freedom."

'Being honest, so far this plan does not seem all that impressive,' said Walker.

"You haven't heard the best part, General. There's one more thing, one minor detail" she said, her voice shaking.

"I can't wait to hear what the minor detail is," he said, with unrestrained sarcasm.

"Okay, Seth, here it comes. The final part of this plan is to bring YOU to Valerion as my prisoner. I plan to tell him that you were taken prisoner by a turncoat in your own ranks who wants asylum."

Walker narrowed his eyes. "What kind of fool does she think I am?" he thought to himself. "There isn't a single thing she could say to make me agree to being held a "fake" prisoner."

JP strengthened his grip on his pistol and leveled it between her eyes.

Morgan spoke first. "This is suicide, General. When do you start making sense, lady?"

"Gentlemen," Megan barked. Here is the core of my plan, such as it is. Valerion takes us all as prisoners. There is no doubt of this. He trusts no one. My hope is that one of or all of us will be able to find Anya and escape Nightwing, the new name of his command ship, and bring her to The People."

"My God, I couldn't possibly dream up a plan with lower prospects of success if I tried," said JP'

"Please let me finish. I admit the chances of any of us surviving this action fluctuate between bad and really bad, but let me say this: whatever the odds are that I could pull this off by myself, with three of us we have three times the chance. Anya has capabilities that none of us could even imagine AND she knows how to find her way home. Isn't that worth the risk?"

"OK, let's move on to the part about Anya, the green lady," said General Walker. He walked over to where JP was sitting and asked, "Is Anya the real deal? Can she find us a new home?"

JP paused and looked down at his feet. He then looked Walker in the eyes and said, "Without her, you know we could roam the universe for generations before finding a home. I hate to say it, but I agree with Megan. Anya is the best chance we have of finding a new home planet in short order."

Walker turned toward his ex-wife and said, "Okay who is the cowardly traitor who supposedly turned me over to you?"

"Who else but JP?" she said with a smirk on her face. "He's perfect for this role."

*****

"Megan, have a seat while I speak with these two."

"General, you aren't seriously considering going along with this wild scheme," asked Morgan.

"Guys, we don't have much time," Walker said. "As bizarre as it is, I believe this could be the best chance we have to find a new home for our people. Ed, as soon as we leave, go find my brother, Max, and make immediate plans to use the space transports that he and I discussed. Get

The People off this planet. Max oversees the move and you oversee security. Tell The People I will rejoin them as soon as possible. Take Pincus with you and hold him until I return."

"Sir, how do you know you can trust this jezebel? Sorry, no offense meant but she has shown her true colors before."

"I don't trust her in the least but if we have even a remote chance of finding a home for The People, let's be honest, we have to take it. We aren't overrun with options other than prowling around the universe looking for a suitable home planet."

"What about me, General?" asked JP with the look of a puppy that has lost his master.

"My friend, you have the most important and difficult role to play. I know that this may well be a one-way trip for me, but I believe you will survive. Your only mission is to find Anya and get her back to The People, with or without me. Do you copy?"

JP simply stared at his friend in disbelief.

"JP, do you copy me?" Walker shouted.

"Yes, sir," said JP meekly.

"Now you two, let's do this thing before I come to my senses and change my mind," said Walker. "Before I go, I need to make a quick call to my brother."

CHAPTER 6

Back in the rebel fortress on Elon, the color drained out of Max's face as he talked with his brother. All he could say was, "Don't take this wrong, brother, but that is one of the dumbest ideas I have ever heard."

*****

As soon as the gondola containing General Walker, JP, his ex-wife, and a large group of Valerion's troops were transported up the tether in a gondola into space, a shiver ran up Colonel Morgan's spine at the risk that Walker and JP were taking. No matter who she once was, there was no way he trusted that woman. Notwithstanding his screaming doubts about Walker's ex-wife, Morgan tries to grasp what made Walker believe this ultra-high-risk plan could succeed.

"No time to waste," thought as he turned to rejoin his troops, pick up his prisoner, and then face Max Walker and try to explain why his big brother did what he just did.

*****

Max turned to his next in command, Austin Jacques, and said, "Get The People moving to their assigned departure location and let's get off this rock. The path is clear, and today is the day we leave this planet. We have practiced this procedure for months and now we must make it happen."

Austin looked troubled and said, "Where is Seth?"

"I spoke with him several minutes ago and he said that we should not wait for him. He will catch up with us as soon as possible."

As Max was giving orders putting the evacuation plan into effect, Ed Morgan walked up to him at the Command-and-Control Headquarters.

"How could you let him do this, Morgan?" Max snapped. "I trusted you to have his back. Handing him over to Valerion sounds like a death sentence to me."

"Do you remember the last time you ever won an argument with your brother, Mr. Walker?"

"No."

"No, I don't," replied the younger Walker somewhat sheepishly. He realized that his big brother had given Colonel Morgan no choice.

That realization seemed to calm Seth's brother, but it was far from satisfying.

Colonel Morgan said to the younger Walker, "Seth told me that you were in charge of getting our people off Elon. Would you please tell me how you intend to get these fine people off this smoldering rock?"

"Sure," said Max. "Let's walk to the disembarkation area, Colonel. I'll give you the basics of the plan as we go."

Max continued, "We knew that if we didn't have access to space transportation, we would simply burn to death here on Elon. Therefore, months before Valerion's mass exodus from the planet, we sent teams of pilots carefully selected space elevators to find the best space transports available. It was like all the space cruisers on the planet were parked in orbit twenty-five thousand miles from the surface."

"Spaceships being parked there is understandable but being unguarded is absolutely not understandable," said the Colonel.

"Valerion had no one guarding the fleet of space craft because the job of controlling the populace on Elon consumed the efforts of every soldier he could find. Seth had a sense of what was going to happen and it occurred just as he suspected: mass slaughter of those who were of no use to him or those who could not buy their way onto Valerion's escape plan."

"Are you saying our pilots just went up the space elevators and went shopping for space craft?" asked Morgan with a look of unbelief across his face.

"That is exactly what I am saying. Keeping the space transports unguarded was one of Valerion's most significant miscalculations, but," said Max, "a stroke of great luck for us. Good fortune comes to the well prepared and Seth had been waiting for months for a chance to grab a small fleet of space cruisers when Valerion was distracted"

Morgan smiled and shook his head back and forth as he began to understand Walker's brilliance. "Your brother is a superb strategist," he said

"Yes, he is," replied Max. "I only hope he has a plan that will keep him alive when he meets up with Valerion face to face."

Still wondering about the details of Walker's plan, he asked, "How did we get so many pilots that we could trust?"

"All these pilots had been members of Valerion's Space Command. But many became disenchanted with Valerion because of the excessive brutality required of his soldiers. My brother knew many of the pilots from the time that he was in the Space Command. When the time was right, he made them and their families an offer of better lives than they could ever have with Valerion. The rest is history."

"So where are the pilots and the space craft located now?"

"The pilots took all the spacecraft that we needed to transport both The People and the bio pods and joined into a close formation out of range of Valerion's sensors. If everything goes according to plan, in twenty hours, each cruiser will dock at their assigned space elevator and wait for the signal to land on the surface and pick up The People. We have ten transports, which is more than we need. Each transport can carry over one thousand people so, in a sense, we have a few spares."

*****

"Colonel, you asked what you could do to help. The people will soon be moving to their assigned stations for pick up. For most, they will begin within several hours. Have your soldiers accompany The People and try to reassure them that the evacuation is proceeding according to the plan. Many people are understandably nervous and it might not take much to start a panic."

"Is there anything else we should be concerned about, Mr. Walker?"

"Just divide your troops into five teams and have half of each team go with the first group and the other half go with the second half. Their job is to maintain order and be on the alert for any strays that might have been left behind by Valerion. We must be suspicious of anyone we do not know, and each must be properly vetted and their backgrounds thoroughly checked. At this point we know our own people but all outsiders must be treated as if they are hostile."

"And if we find any people who are not part of our group, what then?"

"Keep them isolated from The People. Anyone who has been outside in this heat for any length of time will no doubt suffer from hyperthermia at best or be an agent of Valerion at worst. We need to determine their allegiances and whether we can trust them. They will be placed on one of the extra transports but not be allowed to mingle with The People until we are certain they pose no harm."

CHAPTER 7

Megan Murray was standing on the bridge when the helmsman turned his head and reported, with growing terror in his eyes, that their ship had been caught in a tractor beam and was being diverted from its original destination to the main bay of Valerion's command cruiser, Nightwing. 'Valerion gave orders for everyone to remain on this ship after docking,' said the helmsman to Murray.

Megan Murray was standing next to JP. Seth Walker was in restraints in a secure cabin. She told JP, "Originally, the plan was for us to disembark at one of the main troop ships, but after I sent word to Valerion that Pincus had been handed over to the resistance and that I had a special gift for him, plans changed. We will be landing at his command ship."

"How do you feel about Valerion's change of plans?" asked JP.

"It doesn't inspire overwhelming optimism," she replied. "He is paranoid. Being diverted from our original flight plan and pulled into Nightwing by a tractor beam, screams to me that he is irreparably suspicious. My immediate concern is that he doesn't kill us all for failing to complete the mission."

As a show of strength, Valerion ordered four thousand of his uniformed troops to surround the troop transport when it finally settled onto the flight deck. The large rear door of the transport opened and Megan Murray stood alone at the entrance. Megan felt like an insect caught in a spider's web face-to-face with the spider. Valerion stood with a phalanx of his senior staff at the foot of the exit ramp.

Megan walked down the metal ramp toward Valerion. His gaze resembled a tractor beam, pulling her toward him. When she stopped in front of him, he said blankly, "Search her."

"No weapons, sir," said one of the security detail after an unnecessarily thorough search.

"You failed in your mission, Ms. Murray, and you have returned without Mr. Pincus. I have thousands of soldiers nearby who would die trying to impress me, yet you did not. What good are you to me?" he said as he scanned her face for reaction.

"Sir, during the initial seconds of the attack, they landed several people on the space elevator platform and took over the control center of the elevator. After several minutes of intense bombardment, they broadcast an offer for us to surrender in exchange for Pincus. If we did not comply, they were going to blow the space elevator tether and we would have been stranded only to burn to death on Elon. In my judgement, this was a fight that we could not win."

"I will expect a full report before this time tomorrow. Make it convincing," he said through menacing eyes. "Also, I believe that you mentioned that you had a present for me."

"Yes, sir, I do," said Megan as she spoke into her communicator to her first mate inside the transport. "Send out Mr. Powers with his prisoner," she ordered.

At the top of the exit ramp first appeared JP and then, in secure restraints, Seth Walker.

Valerion's appearance barely changed, but he managed a small, nasty sneer. 'Walker,' he hissed. "Bring him to me."

"Ms. Murray, or is it Mrs. Walker still, tell your first mate to take the ship out of this flight bay and dock as originally planned, at the edge of the fleet."

Valerion turned to one of his deputies and said clearly, "As soon as that ship is clear of Nightwing, blow it out of the sky. One thing I won't have is a celebration of mutinous troops who not only fail to complete their mission but then surrender to the enemy."

Everyone not at rigid attention turned their heads to watch the transport rise, turn, and proceed out into blackness, unaware that everyone on board had only seconds to live.

Megan, on the verge of tears, begged the cruel despot to reconsider his death sentence for the crew. "All they did was follow orders."

"In that event," Ms. Murray, "consider that it was your order to surrender that sealed their fates. You killed them, you see, not me."

'Loose ends,' he thought to himself, with a sneer.

Tears streamed from Megan's eyes as the blast of one dozen photon torpedoes slammed into the transport, ripping it into space dust. The brilliance of the explosions was cast into the huge metal landing bay and onto all the onlookers, an effect that seemed to please Valerion.

"Now, Ms. Murray, let's see what we have here. First, let me be clear. The only reason you were not on that transport when it exploded was my way of thanking you for the gift of General Walker. However, do not think that this in any way removes you from suspicion. There are just too many coincidences for me to think of this as nothing more than just my lucky day."

"Take her to a suite so she can rest before our next chat."

A group of six expressionless guards surrounded Megan and led her away to her "suite."

"Your name is Powers," he said speaking even before turning his head to look at JP, "right?"

"Yes, it is," JP replied respectfully.

"Mr. Powers, I am going to have the guard take your sidearm and check you for additional weapons. You are safe here and you will not need weapons of any kind."

"He is clear of weapons, sir," said the guard.

"What part in this little skit do you play, Mr. Powers?"

"My role in this affair is far from noble. I am acting strictly out of my self-interest. The more I saw Walker and his people flounder trying to escape Elon, the more I began to look for a way to stay alive instead of joining with a dead man walking. That is when I decided to take General Walker as a prisoner and trade him to you for a position in your organization. Within a very few days, if not already, The People will be dying of the heat with no chance of escape and I just didn't see myself wanting that for my future."

"Deceitful and scurrilous. Two excellent character traits: Mr. Powers. Let me tell you what I am going to do with the three of you."

As soon as Valerion had spoken these words, Seth launched himself toward JP in an apparent but obviously futile fit of rage. There was little he could do as he was bound by restraints on his hands and arms. Nevertheless, he rammed into JP knocking him down with a mighty headbutt before a guard knocked the General unconscious with the stock of a rifle.

"Poor Seth. He never did get the bigger picture," Valerion thought as he smiled and shook his head condescendingly. "Guards, search Walker thoroughly and take him to a cell. Try to make him as uncomfortable as possible. He won't be staying with us very long."

"As I was saying, Mr. Powers, after you have rested, I am going to meet with the three of you. I want to know exactly what is going on with Walker's people. They are the only group on Elon that was too stubborn to join my worldwide alliance. I simply want to know when I can be assured that they are all dead. They are loose ends."

As JP walked away to his "suite", Valerion, the supreme ruler of almost every living person from Elon smiled and crossed his arms. He was delighted in the cornucopia of ways in which he might enjoy seeing Walker, his arch enemy, meet his death.

"Which one do you think is the weakest link among these three? It seems likely that there is some scheme they are trying to stage to my detriment?"

"Was the lovely Megan Murray lying? Probably. Was the self-serving Mr. Powers lying? Possibly. In any case, all three will be dead within twenty-four hours unless they can prove of great value to me. That seems like the last of the loose ends," Valerion said to himself with a self-satisfied sneer.

"Powers is the weak link. Walker is the leader and his ex-wife is no doubt trying to find a place back in his life. They will find strength in each other. Powers is the odd man out."

Valerion turned and walked toward his throne room. His chief of security, Kord, walked with him, but one step behind, to show appropriate deference. Valerion said without turning his head, "Make certain their rooms are all next to each other in the guest wing."

"Yes sir, Mr. President."

"Also, send an interrogation team to Powers' room in an hour and find out what he knows. I don't want him killed yet but use enough non-lethal force to make him look like he has lost a street fight. If he does not talk, use the mind probe after dinner. No one can withstand the sweet caress of the mind probe."

"The mind probe will either destroy his mind or kill him, sir," said one of the guards in attendance.

"So what? He has the information I need," he said nonchalantly.

"Oh, one final thing," said Valerion. "In an hour, throw Mr. Walker in with Ms. Murray. I will be watching to see their interactions with each other."

CHAPTER 8

The People planning to leave Elon

Dawn would be breaking in less than one hour but the heat was already nearly sweltering. The first five groups of the Resistance were anxiously making their way to their assigned pickup locations. Colonel Morgan briefed his teams. They would be providing protective escort to The People in case they ran into more of Valerion's killers.

Morgan thought that, given Murphy's Law, it would be a miracle if nothing catastrophic happened as the groups moved to embarkation locations. No sooner had he uttered this to himself than the sound of an automatic weapon fire exploded through his earpiece and snapped him back to reality. He jerked the earpiece out of his ear, as the pain was quite severe.

"Sorry Colonel," said Li Kang: "When we were on the way to one of the transport landing sites we happened upon several strangers trying to break into a space elevator located at its base station." I can't imagine the shock when they reached the end of the tether, about 22,000 miles up, and there was no transport to pick them up."

Morgan said, "Disarm them and keep them separated from The People. I'll send someone over to interview them and see if they maintain any allegiance to Valerion. Let them know that we can give them a way off Elon, but only if they cooperate. How many are there?"

"Not as many as there were a few minutes ago. When they started firing, I shot three of them. Beside them, there are three others."

"Good job, Li. I just wonder who these people are and how many other groups are roaming around the countryside."

"Sir, we can't just tell these strangers to trust us and we'll be back to get you. They are desperate to get off Elon, as we are. I would really appreciate it if you would send over the interview team right away so we can get the strangers and The People on a cruiser and get them off this hot rock."

"I'll send Austin Cahill's team over in a hover craft to interview them."

*****

As soon as Cahill and his well-armed team of interviewers landed near the gondola, he summoned the strangers to join him in the hovercraft.

While he waited for the strangers to board his hovercraft, Austin could see out of the porthole that one group of The People was boarding their assigned transport. Within minutes, they would begin their ascent to join others at the rendezvous point. He and the other interviewers felt a sense of relief that the plan, or at least this part of it, seemed to be working.

The strangers were dressed in what appeared to be expensive and well-tailored clothes, which is hardly what you would expect from an organized militia. In addition, their attire was obviously not designed for roughing it in a desert.

Cahill was first to speak, "Who are you people and where do you come from?"

"We are the servants, cooks, and other staff from Valerion's palace. Valerion left us behind when he and others fled into space several days ago. He was about to have us all executed "as a kindness" but was distracted by some even more trivial matter and we were spared. When he left, we moved into the palace, dressed in their finest clothes, and ate what was left of their food. We are desperate to get off this planet before it burns up. Can you help us?"

"How many of you are there?" asked Austin.

"About fifty or fifty-five in total. The rest are back at the palace."

"Why did you open fire at our team earlier this morning?" asked Li.

"Listen, everyone on this planet wants to get off Elon desperately. We were at the gondola first, and then you came along. We were just defending what we thought of as our place in line."

Austin looked at the strangers curiously, "Where did you think you were going to go once you took the space elevator up as far as it would go? Is there a transport waiting there for you?"

"No sir," said Nartha, the spokesperson for the group. "We have no transport waiting for us. The best way I can describe our situation is that we were simply desperate to stay alive for a bit longer. Let me put it to you this way: if your ship sank in the ocean and you survived, would you not grab onto anything floating to help you survive a bit longer even if the chances of survival were almost nil?"

"You make a good point," Cahill said, "I can sympathize with your thinking and I regret your situation but now let me tell you what we must do. We need to be assured that you and your people pose no threat to us by virtue of some real or imagined loyalty to Valerion."

The sun was coming up and the ground began to shake. The planet was being torn apart. Water deep inside the surface of the globe was being vaporized and the steam was either spraying out or building up inside the surface with the probability of explosive results.

Austin looked at Nartha and said, "We are going to help you get off this rock until the first time you lie to any of us or try to cause us a problem. This is your only opportunity. I will leave a pilot and three guards. The pilot will fly you to the palace so that you can pick up the rest of your people. If you cooperate, you will be on a space transport within hours."

"Li, pick three people to cover your back. You will fly these folks back to the palace to pick up the rest of their people. If anyone tries anything aggressive, show them the door. We just don't have the time to spend with uncooperative strangers."

"Copy that," she said.

Austin keyed his communicator and called in to Colonel Morgan, "Colonel, it looks like we have about fifty additional people coming with us. They were maids, waiters, and gardeners at Valerion's palace. They seem harmless enough and I feel we should include them in our exodus plan."

"Austin, I'm sending another hovercraft to get you and bring you back here. We need to get the two biospheres moving toward a cruiser and off this planet."

"I'll see you shortly, Colonel."

As the sun came up, the temperature also rose, and those who were outside could see steam and other gases being released from deep underground into the sky.

*****

When Li arrived at the palace, it didn't take long to round up the other palace staff and herd them onboard.

"Listen up," she said to her passengers before they closed the door to the jet-propelled, flying metal box. "We are with the resistance and we have a way off this planet. If you cooperate, you will move up a space cruiser with us within hours. Any of you choosing to exercise your right to complain or cause us even the smallest bit of trouble, please signify by saying I want to remain on Elon to burn alive. This is your only warning."

Li was stocky but not fat, and she appeared well-muscled. Also, there was something lethal about her, so when she spoke, people listened.

There was silence, except for Nartha. She said,' You will get no trouble out of us. We were unwilling servants to the political elite. We are not the political elite. We hope you understand how we hated Valerion and the others in the council. If anything, we are your natural allies."

Li smiled and said, "Let's get you off this planet."

As she lifted off with her new human cargo, a violent gas plume erupted below the palace, separating Valerion's palace into two pieces. The rest of the remaining building was being consumed in flames.

"That only seems fitting that the palace be consumed by fire," muttered Nartha. "I just wish that bastard, Valerion, was in the fire burning to death."

The rest of her friends celebrated silently, but none of them felt that their problems were over.

*****

Austin Cahill stepped off the hovercraft and ran inside the command center to avoid being hit by flying boulders that were blasted off the surface by escaping gas and steam. Inside, he met Colonel Morgan, Seth, and several other members of the senior staff who were responsible for getting The People to cruisers.

"I don't see Marco," said Austin who wondered where his fellow team leader and old buddy was.

"I hate to tell you this but Marco and his group were all killed by a massive landslide as they were approaching their cruiser," said Max. "With no vegetation remaining to hold the mountain stable, rock slides are quickly becoming more frequent. The avalanche came down on them as they were in sight of the cruiser," he continued. "All five hundred of them were buried alive."

Colonel Morgan broke the gloomy pall that had fallen over the group and said,' We still have two more functions to complete here. We need to move the rest of The People to their transports, and we have to move the biospheres. Those will be our food supply when we get into space."

"One more question," asked Max. "Has anyone checked on Pincus lately?"

"He is being held in my cabin," replied Morgan with a glint of pride. "I have him secured with a dead-man's collar which will blow his head off if he moves more than five feet from my room or attempts to dismantle it and take it off. He is quite secure."

"Since he killed my brother's wife, I want to go check that he is still where he ought to be," said Max.

Max's family had bitter feelings for Pincus so he set out to make certain that his sister-in-law's murderer was still properly incarcerated. As he approached the door to Morgan's room, he heard Pincus shout, "Just get this collar off of me."

"You are not going anywhere, asshole," Max said to himself and dropped his hand to his holster to bring his weapon to the ready. He was about to kick the door open when he felt a stinging blow to the back of his head. Young Walker was out cold before he hit the floor.

When Max regained consciousness, the first thing he saw was Ed Morgan staring down at his face.

"You took quite a blow to the head and yes Pincus is gone. Do you have any idea what happened?"

"All I know is that I heard Pincus shouting to someone from inside your room. I was about to kick open the door when I hit it from behind. And you said, "Pincus is gone?" Max asked hoping he had misunderstood Colonel Morgan.

'I am afraid he is,' he responded dejectedly. "I don't think there is any doubt that he will be looking for a way off this planet."

"Help me up and let's go find him," said Walker feeling a bit unsteady and slightly embarrassed for having been sucker punched. "Alert the rest of the staff and scan the monitors for him. In addition, we need to confirm if he had help, and if so, how many. We now have one more task to complete: to find Pincus."

By the time Max and Colonel Morgan rejoined the rest of the senior staff, someone had spotted Pincus on one of many video monitors. Pincus ran from the cave with two other individuals toward a space elevator, Li Kang's position.

Colonel Morgan said,' Pincus made a bad choice. Li and her squad are as good as we have. Let her know that Pincus will be coming her direction. She needs to be prepared to deal with them, as the situation dictates."

*****

Pincus and his mysterious allies ran as fast as they could down a path at the bottom of a mountain toward one of the space elevators until Pincus, winded, said, "Stop for a minute'. I need to catch my breath."

"Just how do you plan to get us off this rock?"

Before the stranger could answer, the ground under them rumbled violently. Steam was spewing erratically from open fissures on the mountainside.

Pincus looked up at his new comrade and said, while gasping for air, "Who are you and why did you help me?"

"While you may not believe this, not everyone here loves the Walkers. Definitely not me. I have been looking for revenge against him for passing me over for a promotion several times. And, by the way, my name is Mark White."

"Well, Mr. White, it looks like I owe you a great deal," said Pincus as sincerely as he could considering that insincerity was his stock-n-trade.

White, probing for information, said, "I suppose that you are anxious to get back to your boss, Valerion?"

Not knowing exactly what Mark White wanted to hear, Pincus looked at the ground and muttered, "Oh, yes. I want to get back to Valerion ASAP."

Mr. White said, pointing to the space elevator just a short distance from where they were standing, "I have a two-seat fighter waiting for us docked at the space station at the other end of the tether."

Pincus looked puzzled and said, "A two-seat fighter? But there are three of us. What good is that for three people?"

As soon as Pincus looked up at Mr. White, he was staring down the bore of Mr. White's side arm, pointing directly at him.

"You sad waste of skin. Did you really think I was here to help you? Valerion sent me to make sure that you never leave this planet." His finger closed on the trigger and the hammer fell. The bullet hit Pincus square in the belly, just enough to hurt him, but not enough to kill him. The sadistic killer was saving the kill shot to enjoy later.

The ground beneath the three shook briefly but then seemed to stabilize. Within seconds, a bigger shock hit and all three men were thrown off their feet. An avalanche of rocks and boulders rumbled down the mountain like an out-of-control freight train toward the three men.

From an elevated position, Li and her associates watched the scene unfold between Pincus and the other two. They watched through telescopic sights on their rifles. When Li saw White shoot Pincus, she moved the crosshairs of her rifle scope onto the center of the shooter's chest. She thought to herself, "No one cares about Pincus but if someone is going to shoot that dirtbag, I want it to be me."

When the ground shook, Li and her squad were knocked off their feet, along with the three they were watching.

White rose to his feet and said to Pincus, "I wish we had more time to spend together but it seems that your time has run out." He pointed his weapon at his target but, as he prepared to fire, a shot rang out from Li Kang's long rifle, which tore through his shoulder. He fell to the ground but turned his head in time to see tons of rocks hurtling his way. All the doomed trio could do was close their eyes as night came crashing down on them.

"Wounding the assassin was a close call but I couldn't just sit by and watch him shoot Pincus even though both were only seconds away from being buried under tons of rock. We searched the rock pile, but all three were dead," was Li's report to Max Walker.

Max said, "Whatever Pincus got was better than he deserved. As for the other two guys, well, that's just one more reason we must properly vet anyone we do not know. People in your midst that you do not know are always a question mark. Taking that kind of risk just so you can think of yourself as a civilized person is dangerous and naive."

*****

Max watched as the groups boarded their cruisers and began their ascent to the rendezvous point in space. It was both a feeling of accomplishment that everyone was getting off the planet and a feeling of apprehension that the future was extremely uncertain. Walker's rebellious group of approximately six thousand people was giving up a certain death on Elon for the freedom to search the universe, for nobody knows how long to find a new home planet.

The last group of people arrived on the trail and met Li immediately after the avalanche. Li hurried them on toward their space transport where they met with the workers from Valerion's palace.

"Keep the two groups separate," was the last thing Max said. "This way we can interview the palace workers and make sure we don't have any of Valerion's sympathizers among them. Once we are all in the space transports, just one person allied with Valerion could bring disaster to all of us."

*****

By sunset, Max Walker and the senior staff of The Resistance turned for one final look at their home planet before boarding the last transport bound for space from the surface of Elon. What once was a green and lush landscape was now smoldering and lifeless: no trees, no grass, no animals, and no water.

"My friends, I truly hope we are the last twelve people on our home planet of Elon. From what I see, this planet can no longer support life of any kind. All of The People, except those that were killed in a rock slide, should be on transports heading for the rendezvous in space."

"What about the outsiders we found?" asked the chief investigator, Max Stein.

"We came across less than one hundred strangers during the process of leaving Elon. Our highest priority is to determine all we can about them. We must determine whether anyone poses threats of any kind. We will make that priority number one and combining the two biospheres into one large biosphere will be our second major task."

"In Seth's absence, who will be in charge of creating the new biosphere?" asked Austin. "The combined biosphere is his brainchild."

Max said, "As for who is going to take Seth's place in constructing the biosphere, I suggest that we decide to name the only logical replacement, Dr. John Kuhlken, one of Seth's classmates from Space Academy. I am certain that those of you who know him realize that he is a brilliant engineer."

"Where is Seth," asked ten of the eleven people on board the transport as it roared into outer space.

"Let's get one thing out in the open. You are Seth's closest friends and advisors. He is in the process of trying to find a new planet to occupy. He volunteered for an incredibly dangerous mission to get that information and, if it goes badly, we may never see him again."

"I'm not exactly sure where he is but all I can tell you is that he expects to be back with us soon. That is all I can say right now," Max said as he caught Colonel Morgan's eye. They both knew the depth of the risk Seth was taking, but decided that it might be better if they kept those details to themselves. If his friends knew that he had gone with his ex-wife as a prisoner for Valerion, Max feared that they would think his brother had lost his mind.

All of those on the last space transport out of Elon looked back to what was once their home; they could not help but feel a bit of sadness for their dead or dying planet. All aboard as well as the thousands who had ascended before them had to deal with the sense of loss in their own way, as the planet appeared as not much more than another smoking, dusty, uninhabitable space rock.

Win Song, the highest rated fighter pilot in The Resistance, elbowed Col Morgan and said, "Look, you can still see pyramids from way up here. Legend has it that the pyramids were constructed by a group known as The Builders from outer space. I guess we will never know."

Without turning his head, Morgan gave a knowing half-smile and said, "But, maybe, some day we will. Who knows, we might just meet The Builders one day."

CHAPTER 9

Back on Nightwing

JP sat on a bench in a stark cell that was sarcastically referred to as a suite. Seeing his surroundings, he understood that his situation was not as secure as he initially hoped. In fact, he was concerned that their plan could have used considerably more forethought. He was worried. If he did find Anya, good, but he had to start thinking about getting himself and Seth off this modified starship.

He looked around his cell for anything that could be used as a weapon. He also looked for closed-circuit cameras. There had to be cameras.

He saw a camera and quickly threw his outer shirt on it to cover the lens. For a weapon, he pulled a metal crossbar from the dirty cot and bent it in two pieces both with forty-five degree edges. He now has two knives, each approximately eight inches long. "Crude," he thought to himself, "but effective."

"Time's limited," he thought. "When they see the camera blocked, they will be here super quick. Better get ready for visitors."

The cell door opened mechanically and two uniformed soldiers entered. One approached the cot where JP was lying on his side and reached out to roll him over. He placed his hand on JP's shoulder, intending to roll him in his direction. Instead, JP rolled toward the soldier and shoved one of the knives into his midsection. The other guard drew his sidearm and took aim at JP, but JP grabbed his attacker, who was gasping in pain, and used him as a human shield. JP reached the injured soldier's sidearm and fired it at the door guard.

With both soldiers writhing on the floor in pain, JP retrieved bits and pieces of uniforms and disguised himself in a soldier's uniform.

"Now then, let's see what we can do to find Anya," he thought to himself as he reached out to open the door.

The door flew open. Directly in front of JP stood Valerion, flanked by one dozen armed soldiers.

"Well, well, Mr. Powers," Valerion said. "I fear that you have shaken my trust in you. I am afraid you are now of no further use to me."

Valerion turned to his uniformed guards and said, "Take him to the mind probe unit. I am certain he will tell us everything he knows."

The mind probe unit had been moved to the room next to Walker and his ex-wife so that they could hear their friend scream in pain as the information was torn from the medial temporal lobe, the memory section of his brain.

Megan looked with horror into Seth's eyes as they heard some poor soul in the room next door shrieking in pain as the mind probe was turned up to maximum intensity.

"I hope I am wrong but it sounds like JP," said Walker as he held his head in his hands. "I did this to my best friend. How will I ever forgive myself?" he grieved.

Megan winced with every scream from the room next door. Her eyes watered; she knew Valerion, and she knew whatever he was doing, he felt no remorse.

"I have no further use for this one. Throw him in with the other two. I will speak with Anya now," sneered Valerion after he extracted the name of the person the trio had come in vain to rescue.

Valerion was euphoric, as the realization dawned on him that Walker's plan to save The People was in ash, like their former home planet.

*****

JP's limp body bounced and skidded across the floor in front of Seth and Megan. Seth's head still ached from the beating he took from the trooper, but what hurt more was seeing his friend lying on the floor – motionless. Seth instinctively placed his fingers on JP's carotid artery.

Megan asked, "Does he have any pulse?"

"You try it. I don't feel anything," said Seth in nearly a panic to find any sign of life.

Megan knelt in front of the motionless body and searched for a pulse. "I feel one but it is very faint."

"Let's try and make him comfortable," said the leader of the resistance.

"Seth, I feel awful. This is honestly not how I saw this scenario playing out. I was only trying to help." Megan said with what appeared to be remorse.

"I see where they attached the electrodes to his head. I could only imagine that he had told them whatever they wanted to know. I believe they have Anya's name and no doubt have her hooked up to the same machine."

Seth sat on the cot and rested his head on his hands with his elbows on his knees. "Oh, what have I gotten you in to, my friend?" Seth knew JP would go through Hell for him and from the looks of things, he had.

The General's rage was building inside him. He was furious about Megan. He didn't know if he could trust her, and he was really furious with himself for going along with this whole scheme of hers.

Within minutes, more screams could be heard from the room next door. Seth looked at Megan, "Anya?" Minutes passed, and the screaming seemed to taper off, as if the life force was being drained from the victim next door.

The pneumatic door sprang open and there stood Valerion. He had a surreal, almost hyena-like grin on his face as he stepped into the cell.

"I cannot thank you and your little friend Anya enough. With her assistance, we have a new heading and will be making our way to our new home. Early tomorrow morning, I will be back to see how you tolerate my mind probe unit. I intend to render you a vegetable and send you back to your people in a box. Until then, have a nice night."

He then turned and left the room. To punctuate his departure, several troopers heaved Anya's limp body onto the floor, like a discarded bag of litter.

The door slammed shut and the room containing the vanquished quartet was silent.

Megan threw herself onto the floor to ascertain the small woman's condition. She was very small, like a tiny teenager. She was still - very still - and apparently not breathing. Megan placed her hand on Anya's head to gently caress her patient. As soon as she touched her forehead, Megan felt warm and comforting currents coursing through her body.

"Do not look up. Valerion is watching. Just hover over my body and listen," said a voice seemingly coming from within Anya, though her lips were not moving. This appeared to be mentally inspired telepathy.

"I am from the Naroobian system. All Naroobians have telepathic powers. I was tortured by Valerion and told him the location of a planet that was suitable for him and his people. Do not fear. The torture did not harm me and the planet that I directed him to is certain to bring him and his people an unpleasant ending. Now, move JP next to me as if we are both dead. Also, bring Walker. I need to tell both of you the location of the planet that is ideal for The People. Finally, I have something important to tell him about tomorrow."

Megan stood up and moved over to sit next to Seth. She leaned over and whispered to Seth what Anya had told her.

At first, Walker thought, "Oh please, not more of your wild imagination," but she seemed insistent so he decided to play along with her.

General Walker got up from the cot and announced, "Let's just put these two on the floor. They won't be needing the cot and we might." At that, Walker and Megan positioned the two bodies next to each other on the floor with Anya's arm touching JP.

Walker and Megan knelt next to the two fallen comrades on the floor, as if in a silent vigil. General Walker also immediately began to receive telepathic communication from Anya.

After Anya imparted the location of the planet of Naroobia to both, she told Walker, "Early tomorrow Valerion will torture you intensely. Listen to what I tell you, so you will be able to manage the torture. Once he believes that he has destroyed your mind, he will leave you and be on his way. Finally, General, it gives me great pleasure to tell you that tomorrow your friend, JP, will be restored to perfect health and tomorrow we will escape our captivity on Nightwing, God willing."

CHAPTER 10

The following morning:

"Sir," said one of Valerion's technicians, "no one could withstand that much current run through their brain. He has got to be fried."

Valerion put two fingers on Walker's neck to feel for a pulse. "He still seems to be alive, but just barely. I believe our work here is done," he said with a smile. "Throw him in the room with the rest of them and we will send them all home to Elon tomorrow."

Valerion turned and exited the room with his entourage behind him. He left two soldiers behind. Their job was to take Walker next door with the other prisoners. They placed their long guns on a table in the mind probe room and proceeded to lift Walker and drag him next door. As soon as both soldiers were busy lifting the General, he quickly shed the pretense of unconsciousness, as Anya had told him, slammed one against a wall, and threw the other on top of the first. He then picked up one of the long guns and shot them both.

Walker put on the uniform of one of the soldiers and went next door. As he opened the cell door, everyone in the room cringed, not knowing who or what was coming.

"Let's go," Walker said. "This may be our only chance to get out of here."

JP, who was laying still on the floor, jumped up with a big smile. Anya too was all smiles and looked quite relieved. So far, her little scheme was working.

Megan said, "I know the way to the flight bay. I was there after Valerion commandeered this ship and renamed it Nightwing. Hurry."

"JP, I have a uniform for you next door. Don't mind the pulsar burn hole in the front," said the general with a smile.

"Used clothes?" said JP. "Really? Is this the best you can do?"

"Stop screwing around, you two. Do you have any idea what will happen to us if Valerion finds us?" said Megan.

"Lead the way, Megan," said the general. He was still not certain of Megan's allegiance. "Was she leading us into a trap?" he worried.

Megan and Anya went first, side by side, with JP and Seth escorting them - their pulsar rifles at the ready. It looked like two soldiers escorting two prisoners to anyone who saw them. All looked normal, except for the blast holes in the chests of the two soldiers.

When they reached the flight bay, the general told JP, "Go find something that we can use to get us out of here. Once Valerion finds us missing, our old friend will be out of his mind with rage until he finds us and kills us."

"General," said JP, "all I see here are short range cruisers. We need a ship with some firepower that will get us from here to The People pretty fast."

"Megan," said the General, "You were here on Nightwing before you returned to Elon with Pincus? Do you have any ideas where we can find a long-range fighter to get us to The People?"

"Indeed, I do. The fighters were located at the rear of the armada. We need to get out of Nightwing in whatever we can find that will fly and go look for something fast."

"Before we depart, General, let me take a few minutes to leave a few parting gifts for the folks here on Nightwing," said JP smiling.

Walker could not help appreciating JP's pride in planting spectacular explosives.

*****

A few minutes later, a small transport exited Nightwing's flight bay as sirens, indicating an escape, began to wail. The small ship headed for the safety of numbers inside the convoy and found refuge inside the flight bay of a different nearby transport.

A flurry of activity began to develop inside Nightwing's flight bay in frenzied preparation for a search for the escaped, high value prisoners.

JP turned to General Walker and asked, "Would you care to do the honors?"

0630 hours:

"With pleasure," said the General as he pressed the red button which ignited detonators in the fuel cells in half a dozen ships parked in Nightwing's flight bay. The explosion was impressive and temporarily disabled 60 percent of the flight bay.

"Let's send our little transport back in the direction of Nightwing just to give them something to shoot at. With any luck, they will believe we were in it."

"That kind of diversion is exactly what automatic pilot was made for," replied JP with a wicked grin.

As Nightwing's crew sighted the now abandoned transport heading toward the armada, pulsar cannons opened up on the escape vehicle, blasting it into pieces in seconds.

Anya turned to the trio and said, "His soldiers will be here soon. They will search every ship in the armada, and I fear that we are not yet safe here. Come with me. I know where we can hide."

CHAPTER 11

A final count was taken, and all The People safely boarded one of the ten transports. The palace staff made it to a separate transport and was being interrogated by members of Colonel Morgan's security team.

Colonel Morgan was intent on seeing that none of the palace staff posed a threat to The People in any way. They were searched and scanned for foreign devices, and each was questioned intensely for hours.

A leader of sorts emerged from the palace staff. He was the palace herb gardener, Jason Stockton. He approached Morgan, unable to conceal his frustration, "When will we be questioned enough. We have done nothing wrong, and we are all most grateful for the chance for life. As you know, Valerion had all of us marked for death so you people are our saviors."

Morgan looked the gardener in the face, "Listen buddy, you will be questioned until I can assure The People that not one of you poses any threat. We in the resistance have all lived together, fought Valerion together, suffered together, and knew each other well. You, we don't know at all. We don't owe you asylum but are willing to consider it if we believe you will become a trusted and productive part of our society. That's how this vetting process works."

"That is heartless, Colonel," said Stockton.

"Stockton, let me make it simple for you. You will be questioned until I say you do not need to be questioned any more. You got that?"

"I understand," said Stockton, feeling thoroughly humbled. "Tell me what you want to know so we can get out from under this cloud of doubt."

"First, tell me how long all of you have been working together."

"After Valerion's daughter disappeared, he purged everyone who worked in the palace. He believed that some of them might have been involved in whatever happened. Most of us came here after the purge and worked in slave-like conditions since then" said Stockton.

"Most of you?" said the Colonel with raised eyebrows. "How many newcomers are there?"

"About a year ago, three of the garden staff disappeared but they were replaced quickly. This was strange because after the first three came, a second group of three was added. Most of us have been with the staff for years. It was odd to find six new people in our group."

"Didn't it seem odd to you that six newcomers appeared into your close little group for no apparent reason?"

"Colonel, you don't seem to understand. The answer is both yes and no. To Valerion we were work units. Not people. Our existence was very much an endless drudgery. If the six newcomers had been homicidal maniacs with orders to eliminate us, that would have been more of a blessing than a curse. By the way, one of your officers shot three of the six when the group was trying to break into the space elevator enclosure."

"My friend, what I understand is that there are three individuals in your group that have risen to the top of the suspicious individuals list. Their backgrounds need to be checked. Do you understand?"

"We never considered them a threat to us but, yes, I see your point. Let me help you find them."

Colonel Morgan and Jason set off to find a group of cooks and gardeners to see if the newcomers were possibly among them. As the palace staff was quarantined on one transport to keep them separate from The People, they were easy to inspect.

The two stepped into the cafeteria, where most of the palace staff gathered, enjoying their newfound freedom. The colonel asked Jason, "Do you see them in this room?"

Jason asked several of his closest friends if they had seen the three individuals in question but no one had seen them lately.

Colonel Morgan called Max to alert him and let him know that there may be a problem.

Max said, "Let me send Li and several of her people. Just try to keep her under control; she tends to shoot first and ask questions later."

When Li and her team arrived, Morgan briefed them, and they searched for the three suspicious individuals.

Jason asked Morgan if he could bring his two brothers with them as volunteers. Morgan appreciated their spirit and said, "It's good to see you working with us as a team."

Jason said, "We all owe you our lives. You can't get much more grateful than that, colonel."

The group headed for the bridge, which was possibly the most sensitive area in the entire ship. The next most sensitive area is the engineering section, which contains the ion thruster that propelled the ship.

Li and her people burst into the bridge with weapons drawn only to find everything serene. "This place is clear," she said almost disappointed. She was an action junkie.

"Let's get to engineering quickly," said Morgan. They all broke into a run because it was common knowledge that a small problem with an ion engine could quickly become a much larger problem.

As they rounded a corner leading to the engineering department, they saw the pneumatic door was open and they found three people lying motionless on the floor. Two of them were engineering personnel, and the third was one of the three remaining persons of interest, now suspects. But where were the other two?

"Split up your team, Li, and we'll go hunting for the other two," said Morgan. "Take one of the volunteers with you."

Li took Jason with her and they jogged toward the main engine department. At the back of the large thruster, they spotted two men in black coveralls leaning over the electrical panels. Jason whispered to Li, "That's them. I recognize them."

Li said, "I have no idea what they are doing but I know they aren't our technicians so I must assume they are sabotaging the equipment. I have no patience for someone who would damage equipment and endanger the lives of everyone on this ship."

In a bold but foolish display of bravery, Jason Stockton ran toward the two men, yelling, "You have no business being there. Get away from the equipment. You'll get us all killed."

Li closed her eyes and shook her head in disbelief at the foolish risk Stockton was taking.

CHAPTER 12

Anya looked up at Walker to attract his attention. Like a young girl, she tugged on his uniform shirt sleeve. "General, we are in the prison barge where my sister and I were held captive. It is a combination of a prison barge and a supply vehicle. That is why the flight bay was so unguarded when we arrived."

"Valerion must be in a full-scale rage by now. Not only did he lose you, me, Megan, and JP, but he must be extremely dubious that we were inside the small transport that was destroyed. He is extremely paranoid," said the General.

Megan joined the conversation and said, "He will begin an extensive search of all the ships where we could possibly have sought refuge. This prison barge will certainly be one of the ships that he searches."

"It seems to me that now would be an excellent time to create a raucous disturbance in another ship a safe distance from here," added JP.

"Any ideas?" asked Walker.

Anya looked down humbly and said, "Well I have an observation that could be useful."

Three pairs of eyes turned toward the little green being who just might be the savior of their race on several separate occasions.

"What do you have in mind, Anya," asked Walker, who put a reassuring hand on her shoulder.

"Listen! Hear that? That is the sound of a supply barge leaving this ship on its way to deliver supplies and parts to the other transports in the fleet. If I understand their schedule correctly, another one is being loaded for departure shortly. This transport has been configured to carry electrical and mechanical supplies for Valerion's entire fleet as well as a certain amount of military ordinance."

A broad grin spread across JP's face and he reached down to give her a hug. "How many times will we rely on you to save us? What an idea. All we have to do is confiscate the next supply barge and we are on our way back to our people."

"Not so fast, JP. Good idea but the barges are probably too slow for us to use as an escape vehicle. We need to think of something a bit more devious."

"Megan. You have been in Valerion's upper echelon for some time. Do you know the protocol for how the fleet reacts if it comes under attack?"

"The initial reaction is for the fleet to disburse so that any damage done to one or two vessels will be limited to those vessels only."

"That is exactly what we learned in Space Academy. JP, it's time for us to go to work and do what we do best."

"But, General, this ship contains almost one thousand prisoners and an unknown number of guards," said Megan.

"Anya, how many guards would you say there are stationed on this ship."

"I would say no more than twenty."

"Sounds manageable," said JP with a grin.

"But General, what about the one thousand prisoners?" asked Anya.

"As far as the prisoners are concerned, the enemy of my enemy is my friend. Know what I mean?" Walker said with a grin. "Of course, we will need to interview them but if Valerion had them imprisoned, I feel like they might be assets for us. Agree?"

"I like the way you think, General Walker. Thanks," said Anya.

"Anya, is there any place that you and Megan can go and not be seen while JP and I go out and do a few chores?"

"Finding a nice hidey hole should be no problem."

"JP and I will be back as quickly as possible."

Megan turned her head toward Walker and said, "Please be careful," not wanting to show any overt affection for her ex-husband. She learned the hard way that any man whose pride had been trampled would become a stubborn adversary if pushed too much.

Ignoring Megan's seeming show of concern, however insincere, Walker said "Anya, show us where you two will be hiding when we return. Afterwards, we will be on our way."

As Walker and JP cautiously made their way to the flight bay, JP asked,' What do you think of Megan? Do you trust her?"

"I feel like a fool every time I even think about trusting her," said Walker as they took an elevator to the flight bay. "Until she reveals her real intentions, we should consider her a potential threat."

JP turned his head and flashed an inquisitive look at his boss.

"I know, I know, she's not that hard to look at either," said Walker, "and what drives me crazy is that I could kick myself every time I think like that."

*****

When dressed in Valerion's soldier uniforms, the two escapees enter the flight deck. It was a massive gray steel hangar that allowed personnel shuttles and delivery barges to arrive and depart easily. Two soldiers were busy loading boxes and crates onto the barge.

Within minutes, the two fugitives joined the soldiers who were loading the barge with electrical and mechanical parts for five transports in the space convoy. Walker thought to himself,' With a few minutes alone, I could rig several remote detonators out of these electrical parts. Then all we would need is some fuel cells and we will have improvised explosive devices."

"Make sure your pulse rifle's selector switch is set on STUN. When the barge is fully loaded, we put these two to sleep. Then we can start making deliveries of our own to those other transports."

0730 hours:

Within minutes, the barge lifted off and was on its way, making deliveries to a half dozen transports in the armada. The manifest on the ship's computer listed what supplies went to which transport. The only concern was that one or both of the two escapees might be recognized by troops onboard the transports receiving the supplies.

The monumental audacity of this stunt thrilled Walker. "If this plan works, and we live through it, my old friend Valerion will have a stroke," he thought, not able to hold back a wide grin. But then his grin faded, "For what he did to my wife and my friend, he deserves a severely momentous defeat."

The struggle between Walker and Valerion which began so many years ago seemed to be entering a crescendo phase.

******

0745 hours:

Even as the delivery barge was making its way through the fleet, Valerion toured the destruction of Nightwing's flight bay. "Every minute that Walker is alive mocks me," he muttered to Kord. "I don't believe for one moment that he was destroyed in the shuttle that was blasted out of the sky. Send a team to the debris field to search for organic evidence."

"Yes, Excellency," Kord muttered.

"Now, you idiot. Send the team now," screamed Valerion.

In fear for his life, Kord turned and ran to direct the search for organic remains within the debris field of the shuttle that had been blasted out of the sky. It had never occurred to Kord that Walker and his party were still alive after the small transport was so thoroughly destroyed.

Valerion turned around abruptly to return to the veritable serenity of his chamber. When he arrived, the twelve members of the high council were waiting for him. This shattered any hope he had of an escape from the seemingly constant reminders that he was simply a puppet on a string and that Walker was pulling the string.

"President Valerion," the senior member of the council, Ivan Tew, said, "We need clarification on the explosions that occurred in Nightwing's flight bay this morning."

"What exactly do you require, my friends?" said Valerion with a Cheshire cat smile smeared across his face as he seated himself in the chair at the head of the long council table.

The High Council was the last vestige of the international governing body that presided over Elon after the borders of every state on the planet were abolished as being out of step with the concept of globalism, a.k.a. One world government. Globalism, was the philosophy which arose to supplant nationalism and transferred international power and influence from the many to the few. What the high counsel did not realize was that Valerion deemed their services to be no longer required. With them gone, he alone would rule with absolute power, a life-long dream of his.

"High council, let me explain. There has been an act of sabotage by a group of rebels that were being held prisoner on Nightwing. For those of you who remember him, the leader of this group of terrorists is Seth Walker."

"I can't believe he is still alive," said several of the group. "He is something of a legend among the survivors on Elon."

Valerion flashed a loathsome glare at Tew. "He is no more a legend than Elon is a vibrant oasis in the universe. He has been a symbol of the resistance for more years than I care to remember. He violently opposed the consolidation of the states within the planet that we now rule. In short, I cannot think of any one person who is more at odds with our vision for Elon than Seth Walker."

"Yet he escaped," said Tew. "It sounds like the legend of Seth Walker is having an unexpected and unintended rebirth."

"My dear councilors, there is the possibility that Walker has been killed. Would you allow me to investigate this possibility and continue our meeting later this afternoon?"

"Of course," said Tew. "Shall we say the meeting will continue here at twelve hundred hours?"

"Until then," said Valerion with his most sincere smile forced across his face.

0800 hours: in Valerion's chambers

After the council left his chambers, he placed an urgent call to Kord, "Come to my chamber immediately and bring the best ten palace guards that you know. I fear there may be an attempt on my life. I need your best people – understand?"

"Of course," he uttered, euphoric with excitement. In his tortured mind, he was back in Valerion's favor and was sent on a high-value task for his master.

Valerion knew now was the time for the high chamber to dissolve permanently. "The High Council is one, big, unnecessary detail that I would be rid of."

0800 hours: in a private meeting among the council members

As the members of the high council walked down the hallway and prepared to depart Nightwing for their own residences, Tew diverted them into an empty room for a quiet and serious discussion.

"Friends," said Tew, "do any of you share the same feeling about our next meeting with Valerion that I have? We are the ones who elevated him to power, but it concerns me that he is constantly acting independently of us. We all know how he operates. When I see him, I see a coiled snake ready to strike. It concerns me that our next meeting may be the time when we all disappear and Valerion loses all restraint on his ambitions. Am I alone in these thoughts?"

At first, there was silence. Tew felt a gnawing in the pit of his stomach as he wondered if he had been a bit too honest with his fellow members. This kind of misplaced trust could easily be the beginning of the end for him. Ever so slowly, however, they agreed that they all shared the same concerns.

One of the younger members, Dew Yerden, suggested that they find a squad of loyal, special-forces troops and bring them to the meeting as a security detail. "It seems reasonable," said Yerden, "that we have personal security during these times when Walker and his people are running around blowing things up. Let us be honest with each other. We all know that, over the years, Valerion has ordered the execution of millions of people on Elon. Twelve more wouldn't concern him in the least."

"I was the commander of Valerion's special-forces and can get as many loyal soldiers as we need," said Abraham Nardin, one of the senior members of the council. "This will make our next meeting quite secure – for us – and when Valerion is involved, we need to watch our backs every minute."

"What about the venue? I believe we need a place that is neutral ground, so there is no advantage for either side, unless the advantage goes to us, of course," said Yerden.

"I have the perfect place in mind. What about the observatory on the transport containing the biopods? Everyone understands that one shot through the glass dome, and we all get sucked out through the hole into space. No better deterrent than mutually assured self-destruction," chuckled Nardin. "We'll tell Valerion that we can combine the meeting with an inspection of our main food supply."

Ivan Tew summarized, "Good. It seems like we agree as to adding security as well as neutral location for the meeting. Now, one final but critical detail: if Valerion tries to have us assassinated, we must be of one mind to defend ourselves and retaliate against him instead. Are we in all in accord with this?"

There was total agreement among the council.

Councilman Nardin said, "The security detail will be assembled within three hours and will accompany us to the meeting with Valerion. I suggest that we all decide on an early meeting site so we can plan our agenda."

The site for the strategy meeting that the High Council agreed upon was the prison transport, a most unlikely meeting location for an august body such as this. The High Council will arrive at the prison transport at eleven hundred hours and remain in the Flight Bay to wait for Nardin to bring their security detail. It was decided that Tew would notify Valerion of the change in the meeting site shortly before the meeting, so he would have no time to arrange a trap for them.

CHAPTER 13

Li and Stockton

Li kept a watchful eye on Stockton as he ran toward the two apparent saboteurs. She imagined what a tempting target he would be once he rounded the metal racks of equipment that shielded him from the two suspects. Instinctively she shouted, "Stockton, dive for cover or they will shoot you like they shot the two at the door!" He hit the floor just as a blue blast from one of the pulsar rifles opened up on his position. That was lucky. They just missed him.

In his eagerness to shoot Stockton, the smaller of the two saboteurs stepped out from behind the electrical equipment to obtain a clear shot. This was Li's opportunity. She saw her target through the scope of her pulsar rifle and squeezed the trigger. His head burst into a pink mist and all was quiet.

Li called out to the other saboteur and told him to come out from behind his hiding place and give up. There was no sound until Li heard the pneumatic door open. The last of the saboteurs had gotten away.

She quickly contacted Colonel Morgan and told him what had happened and the direction that the remaining saboteur was heading. She asked Morgan to send technicians to the engine department and check if the two perpetrators had caused any major damage to the main thruster.

Then, she grabbed Stockton up by the collar and jerked him to his feet as she started in pursuit of the last of the enemy. Stockton's face was white. He said, "I've never come that close to having my head blown off. I can't thank you enough."

Li smiled and said, "No problem. Just don't try to be a hero next time. The cemeteries are full of would-be heroes. Besides, I think you are probably a nice guy and, as far as I can tell, nice guys are in short supply in these parts."

They hurried past the dead saboteur. Looking down, Stockton said, "Good Lord, that's a hard way to go."

Li replied, "There are worse ways to go. He never felt a thing."

Li, leading the way, ran past the equipment that the two saboteurs were trying to damage. It appeared to her that nothing was out of order, but she was no technician. They reached a dead end and slowed to a stop in front of the two doors. One door, a glass pneumatic door, was open, and the other, a standard, metal door with Tool Locker inscribed on it, was closed. The two doors were approximately six feet apart.

Li tried the handle on the Tool Locker. It was locked.

Shifting her attention to the open door, she inched her way toward the opening with Stockton following close behind. Sensing his closeness, Li turned around and looked up at "her shadow."

"Jason," she said as nicely as her dozen plus years of military training would allow, "not so close. If he shoots me I don't want him to shoot you as a bonus. Give me a bit of space. Okay?"

"Sorry. Just trying to do my part."

"Jason, as I understand it, your role is to plant and grow food for The People. This is an important part to play in the future. Me, well, I am just a soldier," she said wishing she had kept that last bit of self-deprecation to herself. Exposing even the smallest part of her personal feelings to a stranger made her uncomfortable. Despite her discomfort, she felt that closeness could be developing with this man, partially because of his innocence. This kind of connection was something that Li had tried hard to keep at bay because her life was all about soldiering. Nothing more. Li had always believed that conflicts between the heart and the mind could cause a soldier to lose focus and losing focus can get you killed.

Forcing herself back into a more serious mode, she said, "I don't believe he went through the pneumatic door because it leads to an airlock and the second door is still closed. The doors work opposite to each other, and if one is open, the other is closed, as we see here. The problem is that if he went through both doors, the second door, the last door that he went out of, would be open instead of closed to allow the person to return back to the ship."

"But we heard the pneumatic door operate when we were coming this way," said Stockton, puzzled.

"I believe he activated the door but then realized that the second door was closed and that if he went in, he would be trapped. Afterwards, he went to the only other door in the vicinity, this one across the hall from us."

All warmth rushed from her as she turned toward the door. Without turning her head toward her partner she said, "Move to the side and stay out of the way." Her eyes were fixed on the white door with Tool Locker stenciled on it in black letters. Li was fully in attack mode.

By this time, Morgan and several others had arrived. Li indicated that she was going after the final saboteur. She banged on the door with the butt of her sidearm and said, "We know you are in there. The rest of your gang is dead, and it would not matter to me if you joined them. You have nowhere to go. I want you to drop your weapon and come out."

Morgan came over to Li and showed her the screen of a thermal imaging device that searched for heat signatures from living beings. The device showed that there was indeed a life form inside the room about four feet from the door behind a bulky piece of furniture.

Li pounded on the door again and said, "Look, mister, if I break this door down and come inside and find you holding a weapon, I am going to shoot you. Do you understand that?"

There was still no response from the person inside the room, but he moved deeper into the room. Now, he was about seven feet inside the room and to the left.

Out of concern for one of his soldiers, Morgan came over and whispered to Li, "If you blow the door open, I will follow up with two flashbang grenades. Then, we should be able to go in and deal with him. Remember, he is to your left after you enter."

"Copy," said Li, the huntress.

She looked over to Morgan to indicate that she was ready. She then looked over Morgan's shoulder to Stockton to allow a brief feeling of warmth to enter her cold world. Then she ignited several pieces of explosive and blew the door in.

A blue streak from a plasma rifle pierced out the door and burned a hole in the wall on the opposite side of the hallway from the Tool Locker door. Morgan threw the first flash bang grenade, which exploded with a loud bang, and then followed up with a second one. Believing that the grenades had pacified the situation, Li charged into the darkened room followed by Morgan and several more soldiers, all wearing night vision glasses allowing them to see in the darkness.

Outside the doorway, Stockton could hear Li shout, "Put down that weapon or I will kill you where you stand!"

"Li-Anne," said Morgan sternly.

"Alright," she replied contritely.

Thirty seconds went by until the man in the black coverall came out of the room, with his hands secured behind his back. Two soldiers escorted him. He was shaking and had obviously been smashed by a rifle butt. All he could say was, "Just keep me away from that beast-woman. She was trying to kill me."

Finally, Morgan and Li exited the room. Morgan had his arm around Li and was smiling. Li looked up at her boss and said, "Sir, when I tell someone to drop their weapon and all he can do is smile, I either need to shoot him or smash his face. Since you were so close, I did not shoot him. There would have been parts of him all over your uniform." She smiled back at Morgan.

"Another great job," Morgan said to Li as he turned to walk over to join Stockton.

He shook Stockton's hand and said, "I understand you were a big help to Lt. Kang in disrupting the attempted sabotage of the main engine. Everyone on board owes you a debt of gratitude."

Stockton replied, "I felt like I was mostly in the way, Colonel. If I was any help, I am glad but being around Li is like a crash course in living on the edge. She is a mighty force of nature."

Morgan stepped closer to Stockton and said, "Listen, son, she is wound very tight and they don't make better soldiers than she is. It would be a personal favor to me if you would go to the cantina with her and buy her a drink. Help her wind down. She's not very good at winding down."

"I don't know, sir. She seems so intense."

"You're right, son, she is intense. Sometimes I worry that she cannot unwind, and that's not good either. Just do what you think best, Jason." With this, the Colonel turned and walked away. As he passed Li in the hall, he winked at her and she smiled back.

She thought, "Ok, Stockton, the Colonel told you what to do. Now, do not make me go back to my room alone and sharpen my knives. Let's see what you've got." With that, she turned to walk back to the cantina alone. She took three steps but heard no footsteps from Stockton. She was beginning to feel somewhat rejected. Like, she might have misread him. Somewhat sad and somewhat irritated, she stopped and turned to locate Stockton in the crowd. Crunch. Stockton was running to catch up with her and carry out his plan to ask her to have a drink with him. They collided, and both laughed at their collision.

"I didn't hear you behind me, mister," she said, "and didn't I tell you not to follow behind me so close?"

"Yes, you did but the Colonel suggested that I ask you if you would like to come with me and have a drink and unwind."

She looked at him intently and said, "Are you just following the Colonel's orders or was this in some way your idea?"

"Let me be honest with you," he said looking deeply into her eyes. "It was my idea to ask you out way before the Colonel suggested it. I just didn't know if you'd be interested."

"Well, if we are being honest, let me tell you that I would be most pleased to go with you to the cantina."

After the collision, they were both in each other's personal spaces. They lingered there, face to face, for a moment, and then Li said, "Let me go clean up and I will meet you in the cantina in a few moments. Okay?"

"That's a deal, Li-Ann," said Stockton.

Her eyes narrowed, and her head tilted. She said, "Only my closest friends call me Li-Ann."

"I would like to know you better," he said.

She took in his last statement and pondered it. "Good answer," she replied with a sincere smile. "Meet you there in 15 minutes."

*****

Li dashed to her quarters and shed fifteen pounds of body armor, guns, knives, and various kinds of explosives. She quickly washed all her important parts and put on a loose-fitting top and a skirt that she had saved for a special occasion. She fretted about her hair, but then just figured it would have to do. Her hair was short, and that was that. Li had a date.

She made her way to the cantina and saw Jason sitting at a table for two in a dimly lit corner. "Nice," she thought. "Definitely nice." Her sense of anticipation began to grow.

She looked so different without her cyborg-looking military gear that Jason was uncertain, at first, if it was her. He watched her as she approached with hungry eyes. His breath quickened. 'You look great,' he said.

She was initially uncertain how to handle a sincere compliment. This made her nervous, not knowing how to respond. "I'm glad you like the outfit," she said. "I don't know if you can tell but I'm not very skilled in this kind of situation. It makes me feel a little panicky."

"Li-Ann, what I meant when I said you looked great was not aimed as a compliment on your outfit. While your outfit looks very nice, what I meant was that it made me feel good to see you looking relaxed and slightly unwound. You give off a most appealing vibe when you are off work."

"I haven't had many positive experiences with men. My father was abusive and horrible in many ways. I joined the military to get away from him. Since leaving home, I have a lot of experience with first dates, but not so much with relationships. I had almost given up trying."

"I'm glad you gave me this opportunity to appreciate you for the person you are rather than the job that you do. It would make me very happy to make you very happy."

Li said, "Let's order something to eat before you totally overwhelm me with your charm and I say something foolish like let's go to my room."

Jason reached across the table and wrapped her hands in his hands. Both appreciated the undeniable sensuality of something as simple as holding hands. He stared into her eyes and said, "You took the words out of my mouth and I don't feel foolish about this at all."

CHAPTER 14

0900 hours: Walker on the prison transport

At the same time, the High Council was concluding its preparation for their meeting with Valerion, JP and General Walker returned to the prison transport and reunited with the two, lady team members.

The first thing Anya, the little alien, said to the two returnees was that the search team from Nightwing had come and gone. Their inspection was cursory and barely qualified as modestly thorough. "But it is obvious," she said, "Someone believes we are alive but none of the troops seemed too overly invested in finding us."

"I think," said Walker, "the sooner we start the fireworks, the sooner we can try to get out of here. By the way, I intend to confiscate this transport ship and take all the prisoners with me when we escape. These prisoners have got to know they are expendable and being with us seems a better bet than being whipping boys for Valerion's elite."

"All we need to do is figure out a way to deal with the twenty special-forces troops that are stationed here with us. I am sure they would not leave this ship for any reason except an emergency," said JP.

"Megan, what kind of gas grenades do they keep in the armory? Is there anything we can use to knock these soldiers out?"

"Most of the grenades that we took when I flew to Elon were explosive rather than chemical. However, I remember seeing several cases of chemical grenades that should knock these soldiers out for several hours. My code to the armory door may still work so let's try it out and then go shopping," she said with an eager grin.

0915 hours: on the prison transport

Councilman Nardin leaves his transport for the prison transport to secure the assistance of the special-forces group stationed there. To assure this assistance, he contacts the commander of the squad stationed on the prison transport, his old friend Captain Dworat.

Nardin says, "Captain, assemble your people in the flight bay by 0930 hours. I want to give you a new assignment that will be considerably more interesting than serving as prison guards. If this goes as I expect, it will perhaps become a permanent assignment for you and your group. I will explain when I arrive."

While Nardin and Dworat confer, Megan and Walker quietly sneak into the prison transport armory to locate any ordinance that they could use to disable twenty troops. When they enter the armory, they gaze upon scores of boxes of ammunition, guns, body armor, and explosives. "Ahhh," said Walker. "These chemical grenades will take them out of action for a while."

Megan turns her head and gazes over her shoulder in Walker's direction. She was surveying the man, not the weapons. Suddenly, she felt flushed. Her pulse quickened. Walker, oblivious to her attention, said, "Take as many of these grenades as you can carry and we will go to work." He was like a kid in a candy store.

Suddenly, both their heads snapped toward the hallway that shared a common wall with the armory. The two escapees froze where they were standing like deer in the headlights. It was the sound of troops being mustered in the hallway. Captain Dworat commanded them to get into formation and then made a quick announcement, "People, we are going quick time to the Flight Bay to meet with a member of the High Council, our old boss General Nardin. He tells me that he has an opportunity for us. If we do well, perhaps we can get out of this prison detail and do more of what we are paid to do. Make me proud." With that, the soldiers were off to the Flight Bay oblivious to the two escapees in the adjoining room who were helping themselves to as much military equipment as they could carry.

As soon as the sound of their boots faded, Walker called JP, who had stayed behind to speak with Anya, and said, "Get to the Flight Bay and find out what council member Nardin has in mind for these troops. Every soldier on the ship is running toward the Flight Bay right now. Be careful."

He looked at Megan and said, "What is going on?"

Megan said, with a wrinkled brow and wide eyes, "Do you think they suspect we are here?"

"If they thought we were here, they would just bust into the armory and take us. This sounds like something much grander," said the general.

"You don't appear that you are used to being hunted by scores of trained killers," Walker noted with a sarcastic smile.

"I have to admit, this is not a comfortable feeling for me."

0930 – 1000 hours: on the prison transport

Nardin's shuttle glides to a smooth landing in front of a red carpet that Dworat found for his arrival.

As soon as the shuttle door opened, he stepped out and asked his old comrade, Captain Dworat, to meet him at the top of the stairway. There, they spoke quietly with Dworat standing at attention. After approximately four minutes, Dworat shook Nardin's hand and seemed to be beaming with pride and delight.

The two, standing on a raised, movable stairway, addressed the soldiers below. Nardin said, "It is good to be back among soldiers again. You are my kind of people. We are one. Let me say that I have known Captain Dworat for many years, and I know him as a fearless warrior. You could not have a better commander. Because of our past association and the trust I have in him, I have offered you the opportunity to participate in a new activity. I asked him if you would become the new security detail of the High Council. Let me assure you that only a few hours ago, there was an attempted sabotage of Nightwing by members of the resistance. Just because we have left Elon, the risks have not been left behind. Now, I would like Captain Dworat to fill you in on today's operation."

JP could not believe his ears when he heard Dworat telling his troops that they would be leaving the prison transport totally unguarded and on automatic pilot to accompany the High Council for a meeting with Valerion.

"I can't imagine what kind of concern has swept the High Council into this kind of self-protection frenzy," he said to Walker over the communicator. "What could be that urgent?"

Megan, who had overheard the conversation between Walker and JP, said, "Perhaps the council is in fear for their lives. Let me assure you that working for Valerion does not lend itself to a feeling of comfort and security."

"That has to be it," said Walker with his eyes wide open. "What else could it be? The council is afraid for their lives."

"What is the timeline of their meeting with Valerion, JP?"

"The entire High Council will assemble here on the prison transport at 1100 hours. After they are all assembled, the entire bunch, including the oversized security detail, will leave for the transport containing the bio-pods for the meeting with Valerion at 1200."

"I imagine that the most opportune time for the explosions will be 1205 hours. Each person will be able to see the explosions from the dome on that transport."

"We'd better get back to Anya's hideout until they leave. I imagine the troops will want to get back into the armory for body armor so we need to not be there."

When Megan and Walker returned to Anya's nook, she was asleep. JP had still not returned from the flight bay. While waiting for JP, Seth took the opportunity to tell Megan what was on his mind. "I still can't figure out what's in this for you. I guess it is a little late to ask but why are you throwing your lot in with us at such enormous risk to yourself?"

"I told you, I am carrying a mountain of guilt for what I have done on Valerion's behalf," she muttered with a forced smile and a look of regret

Walker shook his head in disbelief and said, "That's not enough. What is the real reason you are risking so much?"

Reluctantly and slowly, Megan opened up some of the unpleasant chapters of her life to him, "Over the years, I had a series of relationships and even a marriage that ended in failure. Sometimes it was simply my fault, as in the case of our marriage. Other times it was that I set the bar so low for the men in my life that they often ended up disappointing me badly."

"Why do you believe you had such bad outcomes in your relationships?" he said with a concerned look in his eyes.

"I've given this a lot of thought and have spoken with doctors who deal with these matters and I am embarrassed to say that primarily it was my relationship with my father that caused most of these problems. He sent me to the hospital several times when I was young for my failing to meet his usually drug fueled expectations. I never told you this when we were together because it was such an embarrassing memory. You were the only man in my life who treated me as an equal, and frankly, I did not know how to deal with that. So, I left you and buried myself in my work in Valerion's dream. God forgive me but I was very good at what I did. I know I ruined countless lives."

The general sat up straight and took a deep breath and said, "You've heard the old saying, fool me once shame on you, fool me twice…"

"I know. I have no reason to hope that you will believe me, but I want you to know that I appreciate the chance you are giving me. All I want to do now is help find a new home, a new beginning for The People of the Resistance. That seems the least I can do after all the misery I caused to the people of Elon."

"I can't tell you how much it hurt when you left me even though I knew it was my fault," she said.

With her backbone stiffening, she straightened up, looked him in the eye, and said, "General, there is a point where a person feels like she has apologized enough, and I have just about reached that point. For the last time, I traded relationships for a career, which was an empty trade. I was wrong and I am sorry."

"Very well, we will just leave it at that. I appreciate your directness and I am sorry I didn't know any of this earlier."

"You could have asked," she whispered with her eyes misty.

A noise at the door latch caused them to reach for their weapons. Slowly, the door opened and JP backed inside the room after looking both ways down the hallway for enemy troops. He closed the door and turned only to see the two pulsar rifles pointed at his midsection. "My bad, I should have called ahead," he said.

1015 hours: on the prison transport

JP cleared his throat nervously and said, "The remaining members of the High Council will arrive here during the next few minutes and will depart around 1100 in anticipation of their meeting with Valerion at 1200. It would be very useful to listen in on the meeting and find out what is going on."

"We need to stay out of sight until 1100 hours and then, after they leave, we need to ready this ship for a speedy getaway at approximately 1210 hours."

"It will be nice to get away from this convoy so we can relax a bit," said JP. The others all nodded their heads in agreement.

Walker asked Anya, "Are there any prisoners on this transport with skills or information that would be useful to us as we get underway?"

"Oh, yes, general, there are several former crew members of the larger transports that Valerion kept here in prison like you would keep extra cans of food for a rainy day. Another person you will want to speak with is Sam Surret, who was the head of the space armament division. Sam can blow up just about anything but, like the others, Valerion had him warehoused in prison in case he ever needed his services."

"This is better than I could have hoped for," said Walker. "As soon as the High Council and the security detail leave, we need to assemble anyone who can help us operate this ship. Mostly, however, I want to talk to Surret."

1050 hours: on the prison transport

"JP, go back to the flight bay and let me know the minute they are gone."

"Anya, as soon as we get the green light from JP, go find anyone who can help us fly this transport. We will need them to help us all escape."

"Megan, as soon as JP gives us the all-clear signal, you go to the bridge and make sure that it is unmanned. It doesn't make sense that they would leave a ship like this unmanned but Nardin sounded more concerned about his personal safety than the safety of this ship."

1100 hours: on the prison transport

"General, good news. It appears that the council and its security team have left the ship. I think we are alone here."

"Thanks, JP. That's great news."

Megan reporting from the bridge said, "General, the bridge is unmanned. It is so empty that it is eerie."

"Thanks, Megan. Come and join me as we meet the crew members. I would like your input."

"General, the crew members you want to talk with are on level 8. Hurry. They do not believe in their good fortune. Also, I believe we have found an excellent captain for this ship."

"JP, join me and Anya on level 8."

1110 hours: Walker meeting Valerion's prisoners on the prison transport

"Ladies and gentlemen, we don't have a lot of time. You probably know who I am, so I do not need to explain that I am not a friend of Valerion. It is my intention to take this ship and get underway to join the rest of the resistance. We will be able to answer any questions that you have after you have returned to your stations and have reported to JP that the ship is ready for fast departure. Are you with us?"

"I can't believe this," said the chief engineer and the propulsion officer. "We thought we would be in this prison for the rest of our lives. We are all grateful for your saving us."

"My friends, if we don't put some serious distance between us and this convoy by 1215 hours, we will all be answering to Valerion. This prospect does not appeal to me. How about you?"

All crew members were ecstatic to be released from captivity. The thought of freedom seemed too good to be true.

"Where can I find the new captain?"

"Sir, she has already gone to the bridge to prepare to get underway when you give the order."

"I'll go to the bridge after I speak with Sam Surret."

"Right here," said a tall, red-headed fellow as he stepped forward to meet the General.

"Let me get right to the point. Here's what I want, Sam. I believe that we need some remotely controlled mines that we can leave in our ion wake when we depart from the convoy. We will be out of here as fast as we can but, if I know Valerion, it won't take long for him to send some long-range fighters after us to either bring us back or shoot us down."

"I couldn't agree more. As luck would have it, this transport has a larger explosive supply than any other vessel in the convoy. Valerion presumed that the prisoners would be locked up and could pose no threat to the explosive supplies. I should be able to rig a string of explosive mines that will give them something to think about."

1130 hours: Valerion in his chambers in Nightwing

Valerion was pacing back and forth in his chambers, waiting for Kord to return with news about the security detail. As soon as Kord entered the room the president said, "Are they prepared to execute all the traders in the High Council upon my command?"

"Of course, sir," replied Kord who was feeling quite disgusted with himself for having assembled ten soldiers willing to murder the entire High

Council. "There are always psychopaths who are willing to kill for little or no reason, much like yourself, Mr. President," he thought to himself.

Kord closed his eyes and thought, "Being the head of security for Valerion had never been a position that afforded much job security. I have known at least seven people who were in my role but are no longer with here. They just disappear. Can he read my thoughts? Oh, God, I've got to get away from him."

When Kord looked up, Valerion was on the communicator with Tew and members of the High Council. When the communication ended, Valerion was in a rage. He threw the device against the wall and it shattered into pieces. Valerion said,' Tell your men there has been a change of plans. The meeting with the council and their new security detail will be in the observatory in the transport with the biopods. There will be no shooting inside the glass dome. This move tells me that something must have made them very suspicious."

Valerion immediately suspected Kord.

Kord said, "Possibly it was the talk about Walker that made them nervous."

"Or possibly someone leaked the details of my plan to them and that made them nervous," the president said as he slowly turned his head in Kord's direction.

Kord did not respond as he felt himself sinking slowly toward oblivion. He could smell his own nervous sweat.

"I need to calm their concerns, find Walker, and then do away with them all."

"Make my shuttle ready to leave Nightwing and rendezvous with the bipod transport."

"As you wish, sir," replied Kord who left quickly.

1145 hours: Valerion and the High Council arrive at bipod transport

Valerion and his security detail depart for the meeting with the High Council. They arrive at the flight bay shortly after the High Council and their security force arrive.

1158 hours: ruling elite together in the observatory of the biopod transport

Both groups arrived at the observatory surrounded by an impressive supporting cast of security. Valerion was seething with rage as he saw his move to do away with the council countered for now. To make matters worse, he was certain that Walker was still hiding somewhere in the armada.

Upon command from Valerion, Kord reported to the council that no signs of organic material were found in the wreckage of the shuttle that was shot down. He concluded, "The prospect that Walker is still alive and hiding somewhere inside this fleet of ships is very good."

All eyes turned toward Valerion. "Still alive?" said Tew. "You have been predicting his demise for years and yet he continues to embarrass us. What are you doing to find him?"

Valerion glared at Kord, and in unison, the council turned its gaze to the chief of internal security.

"Kord, update us on the search for Walker and the other escapees," Valerion demanded.

As Kord opened his mouth to defend his unsuccessful attempts to find the four missing one-time prisoners, every ship in Valerion's armada was rocked by shockwaves caused by explosions set off remotely by Walker and JP.

In deep space, there is no oxygen needed to fuel explosions or to transmit sound, except inside space ships. Inside the transports, there was plenty of oxygen, so inside the ships there was a lot of both fire and explosive sound.

1205 hours: explosive shockwaves occurred

CHAPTER 15

As shockwaves from the explosions reached everyone in the armada, Walker looked at JP and they both broke into unrestrained grins, high fives, and slaps on the back. The fleet was in panic and, as programmed, every ship that still had propulsion capabilities began to disburse and put distance between themselves and the site of the explosion.

"Bridge," Walker commanded, "make haste to move to the outer perimeter of the fleet and then make sure we keep on going at maximum speed. Copy?"

"Copy that," replied the new captain over the communicator.

"JP, let's get to the bridge and meet the captain of this ship. Megan, why don't you and Sam come along too. I'd like your input on the new ship's crew."

*****

From the observation chamber of the bio-pod transport, Valerion and the High Council could see fires burning in at least five different transports. Walker was careful not to damage the bio-pods lest he cause starvation among Valerion's guests.

Valerion looked at Tew and said, "Gentlemen, we must put away our differences and get to the bottom of this. In my judgement, we are being sabotaged by terrorists. In all honesty, there is no way to project what Walker will do next. We need to calm the thousands of citizens in our transports and make certain that the fleet is intact. If I may suggest, let us get together again in 24 hours at a place of your choosing. I need to excuse myself and determine the extent of the damage to the fleet."

"Yes," Tew said. "We need to get to the bottom of these explosions. I have no doubt that the citizens of this convoy are terrified. This sort of threat to their safety brings into question the competency of the leadership of this convoy. You can push people just so much when their safety and the safety of their families is threatened."

"I feel certain that Walker is at the bottom of this. I will find him and put an end to his meddling permanently."

"Mr. President, for your sake, let's make this an urgent priority of yours," said Tew who was squinting at Valerion with a dark scowl. "None of us want to get blown to bits because your internal security people lack the competence to find the terrorists responsible for these attacks.

Valerion and the High Council returned to their respective transports to try to assess the damage both to the fleet as well as to their political capital. As a sad fact, neither Valerion nor the High Council was faced with the uncertainties of standing for election, a democratic process that had been suspended by executive order while the population of Elon was in space. Despite the power grab by the political elite, a continuation of disturbances like the several explosions and the destruction of shuttle craft within plain view of thousands of citizens on the transports could engender a spirit of rebellion amongst the people in the convoy of space transports. All the political elite realized it was time for them to unify for the sake of appearances until the wrath of Seth Walker had passed.

Valerion's first task was to select a new Chief of Internal Security. Once identified, that person's first duty would be to dispose of Kord and then find Walker.

There were always those sociopaths or, even better, psychopaths in every society who lack conscience and feel no empathy for others. These individuals were known to be eager to handle the "wet work" of unscrupulous leaders who chose not to get their hands dirty. Valerion has a list of candidates who would jump at the chance to impress their leader and quickly rise in stature within Valerion's organization.

*****

Walker in the prison transport with new members of the rebellion

Walker, JP, Megan, and Sam took an elevator to the bridge to meet with the captain and senior crew. On the ride to the bridge Walker asked Sam if he knew who would most likely be the new captain.

"I would be surprised if it is anyone except Capt. Maldenado. Her tactical skills are second to none but she fell out of favor with the ruling class and that got her arrested and thrown into the jail with us. Like many of us in the brig, she was just being kept as a spare asset of the regime."

"Megan, what do you know about Maldenado?"

"I heard that she balked at carrying out one of Valerion's more heinous sets of orders to bomb a rioting population and that is what got her arrested. Valerion doesn't tolerate his orders being questioned."

The General was feeling pleased with his choice of captain as the elevator doors opened. He looked around the bridge and saw several officers standing around a long-range scanner.

He said in his most commanding voice, "I'd like to speak with the Captain of this ship."

Walker knew many of the more senior officers in the Space Force and was anxious to see which one around the scanner claimed the role of captain. To his utter amazement, he recognized one of the faces in the crowd. She was, at one time, quite a close friend of his but her last name was not Maldenado. Her name was Gina Franks. However, Gina Franks turned and walked toward Walker with her hand outstretched. "Seth, I am so happy, and somewhat surprised, to see you alive. Also, I am very excited to be working for you."

"Maldenado?" Walker said. "What happened to Gina Franks?"

"Married name," she replied. "My husband was a gung-ho fighter pilot but had become highly disillusioned by Valerion's unbridled brutality. One day he just didn't come home. I asked people in his squadron and they told me that, on the day he did not return home, he was dragged out by members of Valerion's internal security force. Internal security told the people in his unit that my husband would not be coming back."

Megan spoke up and said, "Valerion is prone to make people disappear when he becomes suspicious of a person's loyalty."

"When they took him from me about six months ago, I became uncontrollably rebellious and that landed me in prison. The only thing that saved me from just disappearing like my husband was my skill in navigating space vehicles."

"Making people disappear has been a practice of his for many years," added Walker. "I don't want to give you any false hopes but not everyone who Valerion takes is terminated. Some are confined and reprogrammed with electronic, chemical, or psychological torture if he believes they may be of some use to him in the future."

"General, I cannot afford to hold out any such hope that he may still be alive. If he is, he is under Valerion's control and is lost to me. In any event, I am putting as much space between me and Valerion as I possibly can. I belong to the rebellion," she said with tears welling up in her eyes.

"Gina Maldenado, I am so sorry to hear about your husband, but I am happy to run into you again. But what I must know is can you run this ship and help us reconnect with the rest of the rebellion?"

"I have operated more complex and less complex ships than this for years. This one will be no problem."

"Are we putting distance between us and Valerion's armada?" asked Walker.

"As quickly as possible. You know these ion engines are not like in the movies where you push a button and are boosted into light speed all at once. Speed builds up slowly with these cruisers."

"Captain Maldenado, I would like to introduce you to two of the folks that came along with me as well as Sam Surret, our ordinance expert. Sam's going to begin dropping explosives in our ion wake which can be detonated remotely in case Valerion sends long range fighters after us."

"I know Sam. It seems you meet some of the finest people in jail. Sam and I spent time in the same cell recently, along with several hundred others. I also remember JP from my days in Research and Development. And I recognize Ms. Murray but I must say that I don't know her as well as I know JP," said Gina.

"You might say Ms. Murray is a guest of the rebellion," said the General.

"Sir, while I am Captain of this vessel, I will take the liberty of speaking my mind."

"By all means," said Walker, "unless I am mistaken, it seems that you are about to do just that."

"My understanding of Ms. Murray is that she held a position of high authority in Valerion's regime. Her work contributed, indirectly, I understand, to the deaths of a vast but unknown number of people on Elon. I don't understand how you can trust a person with a past like hers."

"Captain, it is my hope that we will become a people of second chances. Who here has not done something that we wish we had not done? Megan risked her life to help get us where we are today. The truth is, if it wasn't for Megan, I wouldn't be here and you would still be in Valerion's prison. I propose that we give her a chance to put Valerion's world behind her as we are all trying to do."

"Very well, general. That's how it will be."

As the three were on the elevator leaving the bridge, General Walker turned to his ex-wife and said, "Fool me once shame on you, fool me twice and I will kill you. Megan, don't believe your past is forgotten. I cannot allow anyone to take the opportunity for a new life from these people."

"Gee, thanks for the vote of confidence," she said contemptuously. "Is that your way of saying thanks for leading you to Anya?"

Walker got into her face and said in a low but evil growl, "Being right, now and then, is nice but when lives are at stake you gotta be right every time. Now go stuff your attitude."

Megan had no comeback for Walker's statement, or if she did, she kept it to herself.

The elevator stopped. "Gentlemen, this is my floor," said Megan. "I understand I have a room here. I'm going to get off and go to bed. And General, I understand what you have sacrificed for me. I will not let you down. You'll see."

As Megan stepped out of the elevator and the doors closed behind her, she thought, "What in God's name must I do to impress these people? I have obviously overestimated the impact of my feminine wiles on Seth." She wasn't so much mad at Walker and JP as she was upset that she could not convince them of her sincerity.

As soon as the elevator door closed, JP turned to his friend and said, "Are you sure you know what you are doing with Megan?"

"No, my friend, I'm not the least bit sure. All I can say is that I hope she is telling the truth. We followed her suggestion so we would have a chance to connect with Anya. It wasn't easy but now we have Anya. Now I need to get Anya together with Maldenado so they can determine a proper course to our new home planet."

"Back to the subject of Megan, sir, since she appeared in our midst, I have had an uneasy feeling about her. She was like a political fixer for Valerion and I find that kind of work to be especially despicable."

"I don't know what it is going to take for me to feel comfortable with her so in order to be fair to everyone here is what I want you to do. Go to Maldenado and tell her that I want her to monitor any possible transmissions into or out of Megan's room. I want the captain to know that, like her, we will not ignore Megan's past. But, let me add this: I want Maldenado to put an electronic net around the entire ship and monitor any and all transmissions that may be going out of or coming into the ship. There are a lot of people on this ship who we do not know."

JP couldn't hold back the smile. "That seems like a reasonable approach," he said. "I'm on my way to the bridge."

"And I am on the way to find Anya and bring her to meet the Captain. We need to discuss course alterations. Wait for me on the bridge."

"Copy that, sir."

*****

When Walker arrived on the bridge with Anya, JP and several crew members were bunched around a communication panel. Maldenado turned with a worried look and said, "This ship has been transmitting coded messages since we left the armada. It was like we were trying to contact everyone in the universe. It comes from a tracking beacon that Valerion had installed on every ship for this very purpose. He wanted to be able to find anyone who tried to escape."

"Can the beacon be disabled?" asked Walker.

"We have already done that but the damage has been done. He has to know that the beacon came from this ship and he also knows the direction we are headed," said the Captain. "However, I also have altered our course slightly so that it will be more difficult for him to find us if he even tries."

"Believe me, Valerion will send out all available star fighters. We have crushed his pride and made him look like a fool in front of the High Council. He must be in a catatonic state by now."

"Do you see anything in our baffles on the long-range scanners?"

"No, not yet."

"How many star fighters does Valerion have?"

"I am not certain but I believe there are eight," said the Captain. "It is a relatively small group of fighters because the resistance was the only reason he had to have them at all. He had neutralized everyone else."

Walker said to the Captain, "Call Megan Murray to the bridge. She may have information we need on this subject. Also, "Sam, stand by. I need to talk explosives with you in a minute or two."

Almost miraculously the elevator door opened and Megan stepped out. "Couldn't sleep," she said. "I was dressed and ready as soon as I heard the communication."

"Megan, what do you know about Valerion's star fighter group in the convoy? How many are there and what is their capability?"

All eyes were on Walker's ex-wife waiting for her next statement. "Unless something extraordinary has happened in the last two or three days, there are only four fighters that are in operational condition. Another five are in various stages of disrepair and have been scavenged for parts."

"How do you know this so precisely?"

"At one point, Valerion wanted to send the star fighters to Elon and bomb everyone still alive there, however since there were only four fighters in operational condition, he decided to send Pincus and his group, of which I was a part, to Elon."

Walker turned and looked to the Captain, "How long before they will be in range to be a threat to us?"

"If they depart within an hour of the explosions, they should be flying up our tailpipe within ninety minutes. They are simply much faster than we are."

"Anya, please help the Captain with a course correction."

Anya approached the computer screen showing the sector of the universe that they were traveling and indicated a new heading that was thirty degrees from their current course.

"One final thing," said Walker. "Sam, before we change our heading, I would like to deploy a massive explosive package to greet the fighters when, and if, they get to this point."

"Sir, I have been deploying mines since we left the convoy. Anyone who makes it through the mine field I have created will be one lucky pilot but this next package should take out anyone who makes it this far."

"Great work. Thanks, Sam."

"My friends, we have some work to do during the next few hours. Let's stay alert and stay alive."

"Captain, anything on the long-range scanners yet?" Walker inquired.

"No, sir. But I expect to see them on our scanners any minute."

"Sam, deploy the explosive package now. We need to make a thirty degree course correction before they see us on their scanners. If they follow us on our present heading, they should run into the explosive package that Sam has prepared."

"Copy that"

"Captain, let's make the course correction that you and Anya discussed and see if we can possibly lose them."

"Explosives are away, General," said Surrett.

"Thank you, Mr. Surrett."

"General, I go on the theory that if we can see them then they can see us. Our long-range scanners have picked up an incoming image. It appears that there is only one ship and he is closing on us at a rapid pace."

"Sam, do your sensors tell you whether or not the mine field has worked?"

"Yes sir it does. My data concurs with the Captain's data. If they started with four ships, I calculate there is only one remaining."

"Captain, how long before the fighter who is following us is in a position to fire a missile at us?"

"Ten minutes, sir."

"Sam, exactly how long before the ship following us reaches that explosive package you left for them."

"Four- and one-half minutes, sir."

"Captain, please try to reach the fighter on our long-range frequencies. I would like to speak with the pilot."

While the captain was trying to reach the incoming pilot, Anya came up to the General and tugged at his sleeve. Seth leaned down and she whispered to him, "The pilot behind us appears to be the captain's husband. He is severely damaged and in tremendous pain from the torture that Valerion inflicted on him. I'll let you decide what to do with this information," she said looking up at him with sadness in her eyes.

"Sam, let me know every 30 seconds until he reaches the large explosive."

"Four minutes, General."

"General, I have made contact. Shall I broadcast it on the loudspeaker in the bridge?" asked Captain Maldenado.

"Yes, of course."

"Gentlemen," said Walker to the pilot in pursuit. "I see you are making good time. It appears that you have escaped Valerion and you are coming to join the rebellion. Am I correct?"

"We are star fighters from the Elon convoy. We are here to take Seth Walker prisoner and return to the convoy. Give us Walker and you may go on your way."

Sam held up an electronic pad with three- and one-half minutes to go displayed on it.

Walker held a thumbs up.

"Sir," said the General to the pilot, "Our instruments indicate that your ship is all that remains of your attack group. You are no longer a "we." You are alone and you are speaking with Seth Walker."

"General Walker, before I deployed on this mission, President Valerion told me to bring you back alive or to destroy your entire ship."

"Sir," said the General with all due respect, "I believe you may try to destroy this ship. Do I need to remind you that this vessel is the size of a mountain range and that you are approaching the point where half of your fuel is exhausted? You do not have the firepower to destroy this vessel. Valerion's fighters were designed to bomb and strafe half starved, helpless civilians. Your ship is not designed to win a fight with a large, armed transport."

There was deafening silence while the pilot absorbed what Walker had just told him.

Sam held up the electronic pad with three displayed on it.

Walker bent over and asked Anya to go over to Captain Maldenato and tell her that we may well be speaking with her husband.

"General, you know what happens to me if I return having failed in my mission. I am a dead man. The only option remaining to me is to destroy your ship."

"My friend," the General said, "that is not your only option. You can come and join us. You do not have to die and you do not have to return."

Sam waved his hand to attract Walker's attention and held up the pad indicating two- and one-half minutes.

"Give me a minute to speak with my staff."

Seth turned to face Gina and asked, "Are you ready for this?"

She acknowledged in the affirmative with tears forming in her eyes.

"Sir," the General said, "may I know your name?"

"My name is Alteus Maldenado."

When he said that, everyone on the bridge looked at Walker in astonishment.

"That is impossible. We understood that Alteus Maldenado was dead."

"Two minutes to go," Sam leaned over and whispered to Walker.

"I was being held by internal security until my attitudes could be realigned to conform to Valerion's vision for the future."

"Why?" asked Walker.

"For questioning his vision," replied Maldenado.

"I have someone I want you to talk with."

"Alteus, this is Gina, your wife. You must know you are on a suicide mission. Even if the General went back with you, you would likely run out of fuel. Please give up this mission and join us. I want us to have the life we dreamed of."

Again, there was silence on the speaker until he said, quietly, "Gina…. I must complete my mission."

"One- and one-half minutes, General."

"Alteus, you are many things. You are a soldier, a fine pilot, a husband to me, and the father to our little baby one day. Don't give it all away for a mission that never had a chance of success."

While the Captain was pleading with her husband, JP moved to Walker's side and said, "You know, if he hits this ship with one of his rockets, a lot of our people will die."

Walker asked Anya if it seemed that he is going to give up and join them.

Anya said, "I cannot get a reading on him at this time. He was severely damaged by the brain washing that Valerion's people inflicted on him. It's like he is half man and half machine."

Sam said, "One minute, General."

JP said, "We can't risk one person for over a thousand people, General."

"We are a people of second chances but the people on this ship have a right to live too," the General thought to himself.

"Megan, your thoughts?"

"My read is that he shows no interest in saving himself. It is eerie but it seems like he is not a he but an it. In other words, he or it seems like a machine."

"Thirty seconds till he reaches the kill zone."

"Gina, any progress with your husband?"

"I can't tell if he remembers me at all. He just keeps saying he must complete his mission. It sounds like he is reading off a script. In fact, I don't get any vibe that he is my husband anymore."

"Unless he provides some indication that he has had a change of mind, I must disable his ship so he can't do any damage to us. We can send a shuttle after him once the ship is dead in the water. Gina? Are you okay with that?"

Gina gives a meager, affirmative nod although not a hearty endorsement, "That's better than seeing him blown to bits."

"Sam, detonate the package as soon as his ship has passed it. I don't want to destroy his ship but I do want to disable his engine. Can you do that?"

"I'll do my best but no promises."

"General, he is entering the kill zone now. When he has passed through and is at the outer limit of the kill zone, I will detonate. That should disable his engine. Fire in the hole, General," said Sam.

"Gina, try to speak with him now."

"Alteus, Alteus please speak to me. We need to know if you are undamaged."

The Captain turned her head and looked at Walker over her left shoulder. "I won't ask you to put this ship at risk but you know I have to go and see if he is in that fighter. He may be dead or alive. Of course, I understand it may have only been a machine. You know I need to go, don't you? I have to know."

Walker looked at JP and then Megan. They both gave unenthusiastic but understanding affirmatives.

"Is there someone who can take over for you while you are going to the disabled ship?"

"Any of these five people standing here who have been with me since I took command would be an excellent choice. If I had to choose one, I would say Samantha Fisher. She is one very good big ship captain."

"Samantha, can you do this thing?" asked Walker.

"It would make me as happy as a flea in a dog pound," replied a fit looking lady with a wide smile. Her eyes were beaming at the opportunity to show that she could do what she had been trained to do.

"JP, let's get Gina on her way. Would you take her down to the flight bay and check her out in a shuttle? Gina, we will slow this ship for two and one-half hours. After that, we must resume with or without you. Are you good with that?"

"No problem," she replied wondering what she was getting herself into.

Then, unexpectedly, Megan spoke up. "General, if it is alright with you and with the Captain, I would like to go along with her as company or help or whatever she needs."

"You know this isn't a low-risk operation, don't you?" said Gina hoping that she could discourage her from coming.

"You'd be doing me a favor if you said yes," Megan replied. "I know I'm not exactly critical to this operation on the ship so perhaps I can be doing some good if only as company."

"You know, I probably wouldn't do this for you," said Gina sternly.

"I have come to realize that all I really control is what I do, not what you do. So let's get going."

JP and Walker exchanged glances, as in they both may have been a bit hasty in their reservations about Megan.

JP escorted the two ladies to the flight bay and within an hour they were on their way – back toward the disabled fighter that may or may not contain Gina's husband. As they were about to close the door, JP reminded Gina, "This ship has only two missiles so if you have to use them, make them count."

Back on the bridge, Walker said, "Samantha, let's slow this ship down and hope they can make it back here before we have to leave."

"Copy that, sir," replied Acting Captain Fisher.

*****

Gina piloted her small shuttle with precision and dialed in the heading for the crippled fighter: one hopefully containing her husband.

Several minutes passed without any conversation until Megan said, "Nice exit from the ship. Looks like you have done this before."

"You need to fly little ships before they let you take on a bigger ship," she replied matter-of-factly.

"It appears to me that you have no interest in conversation so let me ask how long until we arrive at the fighter? Now I'll be quiet."

"If you look on the scope in front of me, you can see it. I would say it is about twenty minutes away, weather permitting."

"Weather?" Megan said. "What kind of weather are we supposed to run into in deep space?"

"Just kidding. I was just wondering if you were listening," she said with an impish grin.

Gina was beginning to warm up to Megan and was entertaining the possibility of conversation with her. Maybe, she thought, she had been a bit harsh in her judgement of the woman. Gina blurted out, "Alright, here goes: why did you come with me? You obviously are uncomfortable flying in deep space and the accommodations back at the ship are much nicer, so why come?"

Megan paused for a moment to gather her thoughts and said, "I have a lot to prove to a lot of people, including myself, and coming with you seemed a more productive use of my time than sitting around in the ship." Megan scanned Gina's facial expression as she spoke for signs of a reaction to her comment. Megan had made her living toppling governments for Valerion and made frequent use of her ability to read body language and facial expressions in that effort. But Gina was expressionless.

Gina thought for a moment and asked another question of her captive audience. "Do you and the General have any plans to take up where you left off when your marriage tanked?"

"That's a hard question to answer. It's just not easy to read his interest in reconnecting." Megan really didn't want to discuss her feelings for Walker but the setting seemed to lend itself to soul searching and getting personal. In addition to that, her life was totally in Gina's hands.

Megan decided to shift the conversation away from herself to Gina, "Weren't you and Seth seeing each other for a time?"

"Yes, after you two broke up, he was lonely and hurt. We just drifted together over time. We were very happy for a while, essentially just playing house, but his heart was beginning to be pulled toward the rebellion. I never could feel comfortable with the rebellion because of the risk. Valerion had people searching for rebels everywhere and there were firing squads almost weekly for those who were caught aiding the rebellion.

"So, what happened?"

"He asked me to come with him but I just couldn't. I couldn't risk it….Because I was pregnant," she whispered softly.

"Oh my God, did he know?"

"I never told him. He was so consumed by the rebellion and I couldn't take a chance of being caught by Valerion with a new baby on the way; especially Seth Walker's baby son. In my mind, I loved him too much to tell him. It would have just caused more conflict in his life."

Megan - "Where is the baby now?"

Gina - "He is in the nursery with my two aunts."

Megan - "But what about your husband Alteus? Did he know who the baby's father was?"

Gina - "He knew whose baby it was but he was a loving husband. Knowing the risks, he still took the baby as if the baby was ours. Now you can see why I am so desperate to find him, can't you? He was a much better man than I deserved."

Megan - "You poor thing. I am so sorry."

Gina - "I hope you will keep this secret to yourself. His knowing about having a son wouldn't do anything for him except distract him from saving the rebellion.

Megan - "Of course I will. When we get back do you think we could go visit your son? I would love to meet him. By the way, what is the little fellow's name?"

Gina - "His name is Oryan."

Megan - "I believe that you can live with any number of people but there is only one person that you cannot live without. For me, that man is Seth. Even after I left him, I couldn't stop thinking about him. Now you and I have shared a secret that I would like to have kept quiet. Okay?"

Both women had barred their souls to the other. It was emotionally exhausting and the conversation slowed down. Soon they were both just staring ahead blankly and listening to the low roar of the engine.

The closer the shuttle came to the disabled fighter, the more Gina's attention was diverted away from the conversation about Walker to the condition of the downed spacecraft. "Look out the forward view port for any signs of life, okay?"

"I am here to help, Captain," said Megan.

Gina flew the shuttle over the top of the fighter and angled it forty-five degrees so that Megan could get a clear view of the top of the fighter. The clear canopy of the fighter was intact but the rear of the craft, where the engine was located, was severely damaged. The fighter had two seats, one in front for the pilot and one behind the pilot for the science officer.

"Both seats are empty," said Megan. "This is a two seater aircraft and both seats are empty. I don't know what else to tell you, Gina. It doesn't make any sense."

"Shuttle craft one, this is Acting Captain Fisher. We are detecting what appears to be an unrecognizable code being transmitted from the fighter. See if you can determine the source of the transmission."

"Copy that, Samantha?" said Gina.

"Try playing the code over the speaker," said Megan.

Both women looked at each other and shrugged their shoulders indicating the code was unfamiliar to them.

Suddenly Megan said excitedly, "I see a blinking red led light on the pilot's console which seems to be synchronized with the code. In other words, I think the code is emanating from the downed fighter. But what is it saying and who is it saying it to?"

"I must call this back to the ship and see what they make of this," said Gina.

"Gina, Megan, the code experts here on the ship have been listening to the transmission and they have come up with the following. The onboard ship's computer is named Maldenado, apparently named for the ship's last captain, Captain Alteus Maldenado. There is nothing organic on board. Just a computer. The computer is communicating back to its base on Nightwing in what can best be described as a dying person's last utterances. All the onboard computer keeps repeating is that it must complete its mission. Captain, I am very sorry it couldn't be better news."

"Thanks anyway, Samantha," she said with a deep sigh. "It's just that not knowing whether he is dead or alive is somehow worse than knowing he is dead," and her sighs became sobs.

General Walker came over the air and said, "Megan, do you think you could help Gina get the shuttle back here. We've spent enough time on what looks like another one of Valerion's cruel tricks. I just don't know what he hoped to achieve from this hoax."

"The Captain is really distracted now but maybe I could get this ship turned in the right direction and head for home. It seems to operate pretty much like a video game."

Gina was looking longingly out the window at the pilot's seat in the starfighter. She noticed that the red led lights were blinking in a different pattern. A more hurried pattern. She turned up the sound so they could hear the pattern. It was mesmerizing.

Samantha spoke over the communicator and said, "Gina, listen to this. The transmission from the fighter has changed from saying I must complete my mission to something different. The transmission is now saying, "Gina, this is Alteus. Are you there?"

Gina's head sunk into the palms of her hands. Both women were silent for a moment until Gina spoke, "I've got to know that his ship is empty. I'm going to get on my pressure suit and go see for myself."

"My poor, suffering friend," Megan said as she put a comforting hand on Gina's shoulder. "Don't you feel like you should wait a while and think this thing through? Maybe you should call Walker and see what he thinks."

Gina looked up at Megan and said with tears in her eyes, "I really don't care what anyone says. I am going out to my husband's ship. I have to do this."

Gina walked across the steel plated floor of the shuttle to the vertical cabinets which contained pressure suits used for operating outside the confines of the pressurized spacecraft. As she was about to put on the helmet, Megan asked, "Do you know how the suit works in zero gravity?"

"How hard can it be?" she answered with what Megan believed to be her confession that her knowledge of the suit was minimal. Gina placed her gloved hand on Megan's hand and said, "I don't think this is the smartest thing I have ever done but I am really glad you are with me."

As soon as she was suited up and in the air lock, Megan was on the comm to the bridge filling them in on what was happening.

"I am getting an uncomfortable feeling about her touching the ship," said Walker. "Valerion is so twisted that he would like nothing better than to lure someone into a trap just so he could blow them apart."

"Megan, get on the comm and tell Gina that you are ordered to back the shuttle away from the fighter for safety reasons. JP will tell you how to do that. He knows that shuttle much better than I do."

Megan said, "I feel like a real jerk leaving her in her time of such suffering."

"I feel Gina's pain, Megan, but I don't want you to take a chance on getting vaporized if we are right about the fighter being booby-trapped," said Walker.

Megan shared Walker's feelings of concern and followed JP's instructions to the letter. She had the ship moving in reverse when a huge explosion battered the shuttle backward like a fly being hit with a swatter. Megan was thrown against the hard metal interior of the shuttle. When she came out of her daze, she was uncertain where she was. Her first instinct was to reach for the comm and call Seth Walker because the shuttle was still heading away from the explosion – into deep space. "Where the hell am I?" she shrieked in her mind.

JP was on the comm and spoke to her in a calm voice, "Megan, are you injured?"

"Nothing broken, I think, but I am bruised and shaking pretty bad."

"First, you need to stop the shuttle's momentum. Follow my instructions and you will come to a complete stop."

Several minutes after she strapped herself into the command chair and performed a few maneuvers per JP's instructions, she felt the tumbling stop and her backward momentum slowed to a stop.

She heard Walker's voice next, "Megan, you and the shuttle have been propelled quite a way by the explosion. What we are going to do is ask you to navigate past the explosion site to confirm that it was the explosion of the star fighter. After that, we will get you back here. Can you do that?"

"You mean you want me to go see if Gina survived?"

"Megan, she'd do the same for you," the General snapped.

"I believe you are right but I liked the part about getting back to the ship a lot better than going to see if there is anything left of the fighter or Gina. That poor woman. All she wanted was to know if her husband was dead or alive and she became a pawn in one of Valerion's sick games."

"I know," said Walker sympathetically. "Also, I hope you know we are all very proud of what you did for her in her last hours."

"We actually shared a lot of girl talk."

"I imagine that was interesting," he said with a hint of concern.

"Oh, it was mostly just girl talk," she said softly as she looked down, "but pretty darn interesting girl talk, sir," she finished with a knowing grin, as she turned her head up to meet Walker's gaze.

"When you get back here," said Walker, "I am sure you will find a lot of people have changed their attitudes toward you. Your selflessness proved a lot to everyone. As for me, I was very impressed with the compassion you showed Gina. I didn't know you had that in you."

CHAPTER 16

After hours of back-and-forth communication between JP and Megan, she finally managed to fly the shuttle to a somewhat smooth landing in the flight bay. There was a large but somber crowd awaiting her return. All were sad at the loss of their friend and captain, Gina Maldenado. However, most, if not all of them, showed support for Megan because she volunteered to accompany Maldenado on a journey that few others would have volunteered for. There was no celebration for Megan but at least she felt they showed appreciation for her. That warmed her tired heart.

Seth Walker was among the crowd that came to meet her. After she disembarked from the shuttle, Walker came up to her and said, "I'm sorry about the way this operation turned out. Gina was special to me. I have known her for quite a while. I hope she is now at peace."

Before she exited the shuttle, she told me that going outside the shuttle was not her best ever idea but that she was going anyway.

"I bet you are ready for a little food and a lot of sleep," said Walker.

"Absolutely right," she said. "Any ideas where I can find a cozy little bistro where I can get a decent meal?" she said losing the battle to suppress a grin.

"Come with me," he said. "What the place lacks in ambience, it more than makes up for in quantity."

"The mess hall?" she guessed with a wrinkled forehead.

"I'm afraid that's about as cozy as it gets," he said with a smile.

CHAPTER 17

High Council member Tew called out to Valerion over his communicator, "We need to meet again. Twenty-four hours have passed and we would do well to share information. I can tell you that the citizens on the transports are scared and confused. We need to arrive at a convincing explanation for the events of the last couple of days as well as a plan for going forward."

"I agree. Where shall we meet?"

"Like last time, the observatory," said Tew.

*****

At the meeting Valerion introduced his new chief of internal security, Zadorn.

Zadorn had risen through the ranks as a loner and an unquestioning killer. The Chief of Internal Security was, in essence, Valerion's bodyguard and chief enforcer.

"What happened to Kord?" Tew was quick to ask.

"Kord had an unfortunate accident and fell into the incinerator. Sad," said Valerion blandly while checking his fingernails. The High Council traded knowing glances amongst themselves.

Tew said, "We understand that the prison transport is missing. Do you care to elaborate? As the ruling elite of what remains of our people, we don't have a reputation that inspires much confidence among the citizens."

Valerion shot him a dark scowl.

"My dear High Councilmembers, I have always governed by a few simple rules. The most basic is deception. In general, people are fools. If we tell them what they want to hear often enough, they will come to believe it. I have used that tactic many times on my political enemies and you can see how it worked out. As we are their leaders and it is our job to tell the people that all is well."

"Here is how we must handle any opposition that might arise," said Valerion. "I suggest that we triple the soldiers in every transport. We will tell the citizens it is for their protection. We will say that Kord was responsible for posting guards on the prison transport but he failed to do so. The prison transport was hijacked by Walker. In his remorse, Kord paid for this failure with his life, apparently suicide. Anyone who cannot accept this theft of our transport as a futile act of war by the resistance should be considered unstable and confined. Can we agree on this?"

While Valerion was fabricating his fanciful web of deception for the unsuspecting citizens of the convoy, Zadorn was walking around the room behind the councilmen in what could only be described as an intimidating manner. With the combination of Valerion droning on and Zadorn's heels pounding against the hard, dark floor, the council was getting the message; they felt the pressure.

To drive home the point of the utter futility of resistance, Valerion summarized with this, "As you know, the citizens in this armada have no weapons. If you will recall, we outlawed the private possession of firearms by anyone on Elon. Further, they rely on us for their food which is grown in our biospheres, and we have all the soldiers under our command for billions of miles in any direction. We have the citizens where we want them: totally dependent on us for every element of their existence."

"It is important for people to have a good grasp on where they stand," said Valerion. "Zadorn, show Mr. Tew what I mean."

Valerion's new chief of internal security stood behind the president's chair. He raised one arm and pointed to the High Council's security detail and then raised the other arm and pointed to Valerion's security detail. He then brought his two hands together with an earsplitting clap and the two groups marched toward the back of the room and joined ranks into one, unified force.

Once the unified security detail was in place, Valerion stood and said, "You see, councilman Nardin came to me and told me of your concerns and your attempt to overthrow the government that we have in place. I value loyalty over any other trait and Nardin displayed a great deal of loyalty. Nardin will be leaving the High Council and will assume a new role as my second in command."

"But sir," several of the council cried out before they were cut off by Valerion.

"The sick feeling that you have in the pit of your stomach, at this very moment, is the same feeling that I want any doubting citizen aboard this convoy to have. If I could describe that feeling it should be a combination of both intense fear for your life and utter hopelessness."

"But sir...."

"There will be no reprisal against you for your disloyalty. You must have a chance to prove your loyalty to me. In fact, I want you to continue to be my eyes and ears around the convoy. You will counsel those in the convoy against any feelings of discontent. If any of you feel this is too much to ask, please signify by saying that you would like to go for a walk past the incinerator with Zadorn." Without waiting for a response, Valerion rose from his chair and proceeded to the exit followed by Nardin, then Zadorn, and Valerion's unified security detail.

When the last of the security detail cleared the room, there was a deafening silence. The High Council had been caught, tried, but then pardoned after being found guilty. While no one spoke, they all remembered the time when they could have joined the rebellion but decided to stay and help Valerion consolidate power over all of Elon. Several of them thought about Megan Murray and the role she played in Valerion's consolidation of the planet. They wondered how she convinced Walker that she could be trusted because they remembered her as a wicked game player.

Tew finally managed to calm himself and say, "I suggest that we all try to find ways to be or appear to be useful to Valerion. Meanwhile, let's return to our transports and do our best to calm the growing anxiety of the population. It would be good for us to remember that the prisoners who were to be used as slaves in the days and weeks ahead are now gone. We should do everything in our power to make certain we do not take their places."

CHAPTER 18

The Naroobians

Megan was finishing her meal in the mess hall with her ex-husband. She told him about the sad adventure she shared with Gina Maldenado which eventually ended with her death. Midway through the meal, Walker's communicator erupted with a message that someone was calling him with an urgent message. The message was from JP requesting his presence.

He turned to Megan and said, "JP is my eyes and ears around this place. When he calls, I know I better get going."

"I appreciate your keeping me company," Megan said.

"No problem. I needed a break anyway. We have all been going non-stop for a little over a week," said the General seemingly oblivious to the warm feelings his ex-wife was broadcasting to him with unrelenting, high intensity.

Megan was quietly assessing the downside of attempting to rekindle a closer relationship with her ex-husband. However, she sensed that her interest in reconnecting with him could appear blatantly hypocritical. She believed that he was also stymied by his feelings of survivor guilt over his wife being killed in a bombing that was meant for him. She also acknowledged that she had thoroughly devastated his pride when she walked out on him. As she sat across from him, she wondered why Seth didn't chase after her when she left him. A bright light came on in her head when she thought, "I didn't just leave him. I dumped him. Big difference."

"Strange beings, these men," she thought as she smiled to herself. "Why wouldn't he chase after me after I walked out on him. Yea, right," she concluded. "Who am I kidding?"

"It looks like you could use some sleep," said Megan, trying not to sound like she was issuing an invitation.

"I have to admit that I haven't slept much since we left Elon. But you should go and get some rest. I will see you later," he said as he got up from the table and started off toward the bridge.

Megan's thoughts turned to the secret that Gina had entrusted her with before she died. She had to go down to the nursery and try to get a look at her ex-husband's son. "How would Seth take the news that he had a son?" Something was gnawing inside her that made her wish she had given him a child instead of Gina.

As he exited from the elevator to the bridge, JP was pacing, anxiously waiting for him. He directed him to a metal table where Samantha and Anya were sitting. He said, "General, Anya has some urgent information to share with you. This is either a very serious problem or a serious fantasy."

Feeling somewhat removed from his command role, he said "And what makes you think I can figure this out if you can't?" Walker said to JP with a laugh and a friendly pat on the back.

Anya, who normally had little to say, cleared her throat, looked him in the eye, and said, "General Walker, I believe we need to do two things rather urgently. We need to enhance our efforts to find the first part of your group from Elon and link up with them. Then we need to be on high alert because one of the most ruthless bands of space pirates is headed in this direction. I cannot emphasize strongly enough how important it is for us to avoid showing up on their long-range scanners."

Upon hearing this unquestionably disturbing news, the General's first reaction was to be snapped back into the seriousness of his command position. He thought, "how could this tiny being know something so threatening that he was totally unaware of?"

"Anya, what makes you say there is a hostile group coming this direction? Tell me how you know this is true."

"General, your people have never encountered anyone from another planet, except for me. In time, you will come to understand, as I do, the universe is filled with species other than yourselves. The group of marauders that I told you about, known as the Yardak, is looking for a new planet to occupy because their planet is about to be swallowed by a wandering black hole."

Highly skeptical of her facts, he said, "I understand we are space novices but how do you know this sort of threat exists? I don't know it. JP doesn't know it. In fact, no one this ship, except you, knows about the Yardak."

"I come from a planet in the Naroobian system. We are a civilization that is billions of years older than you Elonese. Quite simply we are more advanced than you. We know about the Yardak because our sensors are more advanced than yours and we can detect them coming. It's as simple as we can detect them and you can't."

"Let's say we acknowledge that your sensors are more advanced than ours. How did you know that the Naroobians see the Yardak coming this direction? Do you personally have built-in long-range sensors?"

Anya was becoming frustrated by the General's reluctance to contemplate the possibility of something that he cannot see. She realized that what she was telling him required a huge leap of faith for him to believe her. She decided to open up and tell them all the facts.

Anya said, "By all accounts, we are an ancient civilization and we have developed powers and capabilities far superior to yours. One of those powers, that I demonstrated to you while we were on Nightwing, is telepathy. We can communicate with others by extrasensory means. My family, who does have access to such advanced sensors, has telepathically alerted me that the Yardak's course will take them very near us."

Walker followed up, "All of us are trained to react to things that we can see, touch, hear, or feel and extrasensory perception is not one of these. How can we feel the same level of confidence in this information that you have?"

Anya responded, "My friends, it takes a great deal of discernment but you must not immediately discount things that you don't understand. The abilities that we possess and that you are so skeptical of, are perfectly normal to us. Nothing special. Just everyday mind reading," she said as a confident smile spread across her youthful face. "What I am trying to tell you is information that can save your lives and, general, as the leader of this group, you have no right to take what I tell you anyway but seriously."

Seth Walker was taken aback. He was not used to being lectured by a smiling crewmember who was half his size. Yet, he was having a difficult time forming an argument against her position that sounded like anything but condescension. If her story was legitimate, he was quite out of line.

Walker said, "That is a fair point, Anya. Allow me to ask one final question. Why should we fear the Yardak more than they fear us?"

Anya said, "Let me give you the short list of reasons why you should take me very seriously, General. They are many and we are few. They are a heavily armed raiding party and we have limited offensive weapons. And finally, the Yardak are cannibals. They will conquer you and eat everyone on this ship. Shall I go on? Or does that give you all you need to reconsider your skepticism?"

There was silence at the table as each person pondered the prospect of becoming a meal for the Yardak. Before anyone could say anything, Anya mentioned one more thing, "We have monitored their transmissions for months. We don't know exactly where they have come from but their heading has not changed. They are on a heading for the Milky Way Galaxy and have not varied from that course. Their heading will take them right up our tailpipes because they are faster than we are."

Finally, Walker said, "Okay that is quite a closing argument. Is there anything else you need to tell us?"

"Yes," said Anya matter-of-factly. "When we locate your brother and his convoy and we join them, I can lead you to a friendly planet where we can wait, undetected, for the Yardak to pass."

Walker said, "And I suppose you know of such a planet where we can rendezvous?" he asked mockingly.

"As a matter of fact, yes, I do," Anya said. "In fact, I have relatives who live there."

The General, still with lingering doubts about the story Anya was telling him, turned toward the Captain and said, "Samantha, I want you to gather all your communication people together and start an all-out effort to find my brother's convoy ASAP. Consider this urgent."

"We're on it, sir," she replied scrambling to assemble anyone who could be helpful in locating Max Walker and his convoy consisting of the last of the rebels from Elon.

"General," Anya said, "that won't be necessary. You can contact your brother, through me, if you will let me help you. We can communicate with them and provide them the heading to the planet within the Naroobian system called Lordune which is where we are currently heading. I hope this communication may help convince you that what I have told you is true."

Walker looked across the table at JP and they both nodded their heads in the affirmative.

Walker said, "Very well, Anya, let's get ready to contact my brother. Also, I regret doubting you but this is a lot to take in."

Anya - "General, you sit here at the table and Samantha please turn down the lights. General, I will stand behind you and place my hands on your temples. Next, all you have to do is think to your brother like you were talking to him. I will amplify and transmit your thoughts to him."

Walker - "I would love to see his face when he hears me talking to him. This will blow his mind," said the General.

Anya - "Yes it will, if he is anything like you, but you must convince him to listen and then simply explain what has happened. Ready? Go ahead and think to your brother."

As Anya and Walker were beginning the communication process, the elevator door opened and Megan stepped out onto the bridge. She looked left and then right in her tight-fitting jumpsuit. She was dressed provocatively to impress Walker.

When JP saw her, his eyes widened and he thought, "The former Mrs. Walker is looking quite alluring."

"Wow, I've never seen this place so dark? Don't tell me there is a séance going on," Megan said as she chortled to herself.

JP took her by the arm and led her to a distant part of the bridge. There, he whispered to her what was taking place.

After JP finished telling her what was going on she said, "My God, this is fantasy. And tell me again why are we supposed to believe that she has such powers?"

JP - "Megan, all I can say is that this foray with your ex-husband has literally been unbelievable, every minute, from the start until right now. He thinks on a different level than most of us and he trusts her. From what I have seen, our choices are to give her the benefit of the doubt or just wait for an army of cannibals behind us to catch us and see what happens then."

"Any thoughts, Megan?" asked JP.

"No, nothing that trumps an army of cannibals," she replied.

JP - "We will know shortly. If General Walker is able to communicate with his brother, that will all but eliminate Anya's credibility gap. I hope it works because otherwise we have no idea how we are going to locate the rest of our people."

The light from the elevator shown again into the darkened bridge and out stepped Anya's sister, Vanya. JP motioned her over to where he and Megan were standing. Vanya looked like a twin of Anya except her hair was blond.

She appeared anxious. "JP, whatever you are doing here we need to speed it up. My father estimates that this ship will be in the Yardak's scanner range within forty-eight hours or less. After that, it is just a matter of two or three days before they catch up with us. They are coming toward us much faster than we are going away from them which means, of course, they will overtake us at some time."

Shortly after Vanya arrived on the bridge, Anya removed her hands from Walker's temples and stepped around to Walker's side to look him in the face. "That wasn't so bad. Was it?"

Walker smiled, ran his fingers through his hair, and said, "Wow. I was just talking to my brother. It is so hard to imagine experiencing anything like that. Within the next few minutes Max will be changing his heading toward Lordune. Both his group and this ship should be on Lordune within thirty-six hours."

"This seems too good to be true," JP said.

Walker said, "Like Anya has been saying, what may seem like a miracle to us is just everyday communication to her people. The Yardak notwithstanding, I, for one, am a believer in what this young lady has been trying to tell us. I'm sorry I gave her such a hard time."

Anya - "No need to apologize. You were simply thinking within the bounds of what you know to be true. We Naroobians just have a few extra capabilities than you have yet to develop."

JP - "General, you need to meet Anya's sister, Vanya. She has come with some disturbing news."

Vanya - "General, my father has given me an update. He now calculates that the Yardak are now about thirty-six hours from being able to detect this ship on their long-range scanner. He urges that we make all due haste to Lordune or they will detect us and we may lead them directly to Lordune."

Walker - "Let's at least be smart enough to take your father's advice."

"JP, please locate Sam and have him meet us here on the bridge. We need a little insurance policy in case our cannibal friends get too close."

General Walker walked over to where Anya and Vanya were talking with Samantha. He said, "Ladies, I can't find Lordune on the star chart. Why not?"

"General, if you can't find it neither can the Yardak. That's a good thing, don't you think?" said Vanya with an impish smile.

The general shot a glance at Anya and said, "This is no time for games. I need to know why I can't find Lordune on this chart."

"Vanya, this is serious. Stop showing off or go back to your room," said Anya in an older sister kind of tone. "General, Lordune isn't on the map because it is hidden. Lordune is a safe place for the Naroobians to go and not worry about being found by extraterrestrials. It is hidden by a cloaking device which conceals the entire planet from being seen visually or detected by scanning devices."

Walker - "The entire planet is hidden from detection?" he asked with amazement.

Anya - "We have kept it hidden for millions of years using light bending technologies as well as other advanced electronic shielding technologies."

Samantha walked up to Walker and looked up at him with a serious look on her face, "General, Anya tells me that in order to stay out of the Yardak's sensor range, and we will need more speed. Unfortunately, we are traveling at flank speed now. What I am telling you is that unless we can think of something creative, we will be in their scanner range soon, very soon."

"I thought Anya's father just told us we had about thirty-six hours," said JP.

"That thirty-six hours was estimated with their speed, which was still faster than ours, and our speed remaining constant. Apparently, the Yardak have increased their speed for some unknown reason."

Walker gestured for Anya to come over so he could ask her a question quietly. He was concerned that their discussion might panic the crew. He leaned over and spoke to her softly, "Anya, is there any way that you can eavesdrop telepathically on the Yardak commander and listen in on what is going on in his head?"

Anya - "My father just told me that the chatter among the ships in the Yardak fleet is intensifying. As soon as he detected the increase in their communications, he sought to probe the commander's mind and, as you might have guessed, they have detected us on their ultra-long-range scanners. They have increased their speed so they can get close enough to determine if we can be easily defeated and at what cost to themselves."

Walker had hoped that would not be the answer. "Why are they able to see us but we cannot see them?" he asked, already worried he knew the answer.

"The simple answer is that their scanners are better than ours. Fortunately, the Naroobian technology is more advanced than the Yardak's so now, for what it's worth, we know we are being stalked."

Hearing what Anya said, the other four stared at each other in disbelief but disbelief soon turned into dejection. Walker stepped away from the group and began pacing around the bridge. He was searching for answers to questions that had never been asked, or even contemplated, before.

"I can't believe these people have endured so much and now that safety is within our grasp we find ourselves fleeing a gang of cannibals," Walker thought to himself with his head down. "They look to me for leadership and now all they have is the fear of imminent annihilation." He was miserable and the unfamiliar comfort of self-pity was growing strong within him.

JP only had to look at the general to know he was in anguish. He walked over to his friend and put his hand on Walker's shoulder.

"Thanks," he said to JP. "This is the kind of feeling you get in the pit of your stomach when you think everything is going right but then you turn around and the enemy has you in their crosshairs."

Reading their body language, Megan walked over to where the two were standing, put her hands on her hips, looked them in the eye, and said, "You look like you have lost the battle before it started. In this universe, there are two kinds of beings. One group is the hunters and the other group is the hunted. Sometime the only difference between the two is attitude. You two better consider an attitude adjustment or there will be widespread panic on this ship. If we have to fight the Yardak, we'll fight. If you remember, we have an armory full of weapons with us."

Walker and JP exchanged guilty glances at each other.

"I think she makes a good point," said JP.

"Damn right she does. We owe these people our best and moping around when the going gets tough doesn't measure up to our best," agreed Walker. "Megan, thank you for shaking some sense into us. We owe you for that."

Walker looked at his ex-wife and allowed himself to feel some of the feelings he had for her before she left him. The hurt he felt was still there but now it was complicated by the feeling of caring and memories of the romance he held for her before she left. The wall he had erected to keep his feelings for her out of his mind had new cracks in it.

Walker looked her in the face and said, "Maybe we should talk more when we reach Lordune. Okay?"

It was all Megan could do not to tell Seth about his son but now did not feel like the correct time if they were to survive. "Right now, let's focus on staying alive," she said. "We can talk later."

Walker - Shifting back into command mode, Walker turned to Samantha and said, "We know a couple of things for sure. We know that we are on the fastest course to the safety of Lordune. But we also know that the Yardak are on the same course and it is simple mathematics that they will overtake us before we reach safety. We need to change course and try to evade them or we could lead them directly to Lordune. Captain, unless you have a better idea, make that course change immediately."

Walker - "JP, where is Sam?"

JP - "He is already in the process of completing three mega bombs."

Walker - "Good. I've got an idea of what to do with those explosives."

Walker - "JP, here's the plan. Go to Sam and rig two of the explosive packages to be deployed directly at the Yardak at high speed from our rear launch tubes. Next, rig one of the shuttles with the most potent bomb Sam has ever constructed and launch that shuttle directly toward the Yardak fleet. Hopefully the shuttle will serve as a distraction for them to focus on and they won't see the smaller projectiles coming at them. If we are lucky, maybe they will be so intent on our course correction they will just overlook the three devices. Make sure we can remotely detonate them."

Walker - "Next, Anya, how soon before the main group from Elon arrives on Lordune? By my calculations, they should arrive within a day."

Walker - "Finally, Megan, we don't want to panic The People unnecessarily but there may come a time when we will have to tell them that we may soon come under attack and that the attackers may try to board this ship. When that time comes, you and I will try to organize and arm them to repel the Yardak.

Sam called General Walker from the flight bay, "Sir, we have fired the first two explosives at the Yardak fleet. Finally, we are ready to launch the shuttle carrying the final explosive at them."

Walker – "Launch when ready."

Sam – "The shuttle is away, General."

CHAPTER 19

General Walker motioned for Anya to accompany him to a private office adjacent to the bridge.

"Anya, I need for you to ask your father for a final update on the Yardak's state of mind regarding an attack on this ship. I need to know if they intend to take lethal action against us because I have launched several explosive devices at their fleet any one of which could cause substantial damage. If they do not intend to do us harm, I need to know that so I can have the bombs disarmed."

"Let's both speak with my father. His name is Eli. Please sit down and I will communicate with him telepathically through you."

"Father, General Walker needs to be reassured as to the intentions of the Yardak toward the people on this ship. Do they intend to attack this ship?"

"General, I appreciate your concern but let me now allay any such doubts you may have as to the intentions of the Yardak. They are indeed preparing to attack your vessel and I can tell you that the main concern of their commander is "not to destroy the meat." They will not attack with rockets as that might vaporize their prize. Instead, they plan to send about one thousand soldiers aboard to harvest every living creature aboard your ship."

"Eli, just to be clear," Walker said reluctantly, "we are the meat? Correct?"

"Yes general, you are the meat that they want. They look at your ship as a flying banquet, much like a cat and mouse with the mouse being out of escape options."

"I would like to send our two shuttles to Lordune when our flight path takes us closest to the planet. I plan to send women and children and I will include your daughters. It is the least I can do for all your help."

"Whether they come or stay is their choice but, as a father, I appreciate the gesture."

"As soon as the shuttles are away to Lordune, I will turn the ship away from your planet and lead the Yardak away from you. Otherwise, I fear I will draw their attention to your planet."

"A brave and selfless decision, my friend. I hope one day perhaps we will meet. In the meantime, I will take care of your people as if they were my own. God's speed."

"Thank you, Eli. Walker out."

"Anya, you must go with the women and children. I won't have you sacrifice yourself when you are so close to home."

Anya smiled demurely and said, "We'll see." Then she looked into his face, as if she was emboldening herself to say something dramatic, and said, "Seth, you need to talk with Megan. She is carrying a secret which she wants badly to tell you. Do it soon."

Curious about what the secret might be, he said, "Thank you, Anya, I will."

Walker stepped outside the conference room and summoned JP. "Please gather the senior staff and representatives from The People. I need to talk with them here in twenty minutes."

"Megan, please join me in the small conference room for a minute or two?"

Megan walked briskly to the door to the conference room and entered. Seth was standing looking out the window at the stars, enjoying a moment of calm distraction between never-ending crises.

Without turning around, Walker said, "Megan, Anya told me that there was something important you wanted to tell me. Is now a good time to unburden yourself?" He turned toward her, recognizing her very feminine features, and thought thoughts that he had not lately allowed himself to think.

Before Megan answered she thought to herself, "How in the world did Anya know this? Oh my God, she reads minds. I forgot that little detail."

"No, Seth, this is not the best time I can think of to tell you my secret but it seems that our time may be indeed be limited so I had best tell you now." She couldn't look him in the eye when she started speaking because she didn't want to see the look on his face if he took the news badly. She took a deep breath, "Seth, you had a son with Gina that she never told you about. She said you were always too busy and she also couldn't find the right time to tell you. She confided this to me a few minutes before she died."

"And why do you feel this is such a good time to tell me this little bit of news, Megan?"

"Because he is on this ship and I thought you might want to know before we encounter the Yardak. I am sorry but I also kept waiting for the right time to tell you, but it just never seemed to come. I am sorry, Seth. I hope this isn't one more thing I have messed up for you."

She couldn't hold back the tears no matter how hard she tried.

Walker was stunned as much by her reaction as he was with the news.

He walked over to her and took her in his arms. "Megan, there may be plenty of reasons for tears but not telling me this until now isn't one of them. As I look back, I am the reason you did much of what you did, not you. And poor Gina, my dear God, how could I be so self-absorbed? This seems to be a lesson that I should have learned years ago but I didn't until now."

Megan looked up at him, reached around his neck, and drew his head to hers; they locked in a gentle, lingering kiss. After the kiss, Walker blurted out,

"Have you seen him? How old is he? What is his name?"

"I'll take you to see him as soon as you like," she said pulling him down for another kiss, this one more passionate than the one before.

"Megan, I've got to address the crew in a few minutes. One thing I want to tell them is that I am going to send as many women and children as possible off in shuttles to Lordune. The rest of us will decoy the Yardak away from the hidden planet. I would like for you to take my son to Lordune."

"Seth, I need to tell you that I will never leave you again. I did that once and have regretted it every day since then. I am staying with you. I can fight for my people. And for the man I have always loved."

"We will have to talk about this later, after the meeting. I hope you will reconsider taking young Mr. Walker to safety with you though. Do you think you could tell me his name so I don't have to keep calling him Mr. Walker?"

"His name is Oryan. Let's get to the meeting."

*****

Megan stepped out of the door into the bridge, followed by Seth. The bridge was filled with adults as JP had urged them to attend. Megan started to join the crowd but Walker took her arm and said, "Please stay here with me."

"My friends, as you have heard, we are involved in a deadly cat and mouse game with a vicious band of space predators. At one time we believed that we could outrun them but their space fleet is faster than ours. It seems that there will come a time when we must stand and fight them. Before that happens, however, we will send our last two shuttles with as many women and children as possible to the safety of the planet Lordune. There they will join with my brother Max and the remainder of the rebellion from Elon. The shuttles will be leaving in four hours. You will decide with the captain as to who will be leaving us. This is a serious matter and those who remain on this ship will be in grave danger. There will be further instructions to follow. God's blessings to us all."

The crowd of adults was stunned but not surprised. There had been rumors for several hours but the reality of one's own mortality is always a shock.

One man in the crowd shouted out, "Why can't we just go to Lordune? Wasn't that the original plan?"

When Megan saw the man shouting and waving his fist, she froze. It was someone from her past when she worked for Valerion toppling governments. What made her blood run cold was that the protester in the crowd had worked for her. He had been one of her professional protesters whose job was to incite the crowd to violence against the authorities.

She suddenly wished she had somewhere else to be.

Walker, who had been waiting for that question, replied, "Our pursuers are close enough to see this ship on their scanners. If they can see us now and we suddenly disappear, I must believe that would make them suspicious enough to come searching for us. I cannot take the chance that they could find the hidden planet and bring destruction to everyone there. I will not endanger the many to save a few. We simply must lead them away from Lordune."

"Sounds like a personal problem," said the man in the crowd who now had joined with three other vociferous protesters. "We're not part of your rebellion."

Walker turned and whispered to Megan, "Tell JP to watch my back." Then he walked into the crowd until he was face to face with the loudest of the protesters. "Mister, I don't know who you are but until we rescued you several days ago, you were a slave on Valerion's prison ship. Now, at least you have a chance for freedom. With Valerion, you had no chance except a lifetime of servitude and probable death. With us, you have a chance to start a new life. Here's the bottom line: women and children first. Everyone else gets off this ship when I say so. Understand?"

The protester who Seth faced down was lost for an intelligent response and drew back his fist to swing at the General. Walker anticipated the move and instinctively blocked the swing with his left forearm then jabbed him hard in the neck which brought the protester to his knees, gasping for air. A friend of the downed protester reached inside his waistband for a piece of metal pipe. He was going to slug Seth from behind when JP shoved a gun to his ear and told him, "If I pull this trigger, even your mother won't be able to identify you." The coward swallowed hard and dropped the pipe on the floor with a clank.

"JP, let's gather these four up and escort them to the jail cells where Valerion had them stored. The rest of you, now hear this. Women and children off this ship, men stay with me and fight or sit in your jail cells and wait to see the outcome of the fight. Any questions?"

"Samantha, clear the bridge and seal it. Let no one on the bridge except your staff, JP, Sam, Megan, Anya, Vanya, or me."

"Nothing like a little bad news to let you know who your real friends are," smirked JP.

"They are scared. I understand that but my first responsibility is to The People. The folks on this ship never chose to join the revolution and in large part, it shows. I guess I'd hate me too if I were one of these men. The truth is that I am not running for election and I don't care what they want."

After locking the four protesters securely in the cells, Walker armed himself and his party. "Sam, it looks like your little creations are all that stand in the way of the Yardak. How soon before the first two explosives get to the Yardak fleet?"

"Unless they are sighted and destroyed, they will be in the enemy fleet in forty-five minutes."

"Sam, you and JP meet me on the bridge in thirty minutes. Megan and I have somewhere to go until then. And JP, thanks for watching my back - again."

"Megan, let's go meet Mr. Walker."

CHAPTER 20

When Seth and Megan got off the elevator on the children's level, it was noisy like any school lunch room. It was pandemonium.

"How do you find anyone in this chaos, Meg?"

"He has two aunts that are with him constantly. Here comes one of the aunts now."

"General, I thought you would be down here sooner or later. My name is Grace, I am Gina's sister. Let's take you over to where Ryan is playing with his other aunt, Suzanne. And, General, we are very grateful that you saved us from Valerion."

"Believe me, I am in your debt for watching after Ryan. Thank you from the bottom of my heart," he said placing his right hand over his heart and bowing his head as a show of veneration and gratitude.

"I believe they are in this room with the older children," said Aunt Grace as she directed them toward the door.

The closer she got to the door, the slower Seth walked. He looked back, over his shoulder, and whispered to Megan, "Don't we have somewhere we need to be now?" He was nervous as a cat in a lightning storm at the thought of meeting his son for the first time.

Megan placed her hand in the middle of his back and pushed him gently. "Get moving. This is where we are supposed to be now, sir," she replied smiling. She really enjoyed seeing Seth nervous for the first time.

"Well, sir, here he is. Four years old but he is big enough to be five or six. He is the one with the blond hair."

"Can I meet him?"

"Of course, but, General, I must tell you that Gina never told him about you. The only father he has ever known is Gina's husband, Alteus Maldenado. I would take it slow with him if I were you."

"Agreed," said Walker.

A few minutes went by and Walker and Megan said their goodbyes and headed back to the bridge.

"That went well," said Walker beaming with pride at his performance with the four-year-old.

"I don't mean to burst your bubble but do you realize that Ryan did most of the talking. You just stood there smiling and staring at him."

"Okay, you could be right. I'll have to try that again. Maybe I can think of something more to say than nice to meet you."

Megan couldn't contain her smile at Seth's awkwardness with the little fellow. She didn't remember ever seeing him at a loss for words. It warmed her heart but then she remembered that they were in the middle of a fight for their lives. It was a nice break from the tension.

*****

Upon exiting the elevator door to the bridge, the first thing Walker did was ask, "Where is Anya. We will need her to keep in touch with her father so we can monitor the Yardak."

Back in full commander mode, Walker began issuing orders and setting priorities in preparation for their best chance at survival against the Yardak.

"Sam, how long before the first of the devices is in contact with the Yardak's command ship?"

"By my calculations, eight minutes, sir."

Anya, who had been in quiet communication with her father, jumped to her feet and shouted for the General's attention. "General, there is a new frenzy of communication among the commanders in the Yardak fleet. The chatter is very intense and my father believes that the fleet is being recalled. The black hole that was a possible threat to their planet has become an imminent threat. The fleet is needed to rescue as many of the population as possible."

"Are you saying that they are calling off the attack on this ship?"

"Not exactly. The Yardak fleet commander, whose name is Rak, is considering delaying his return home in order to take on provisions."

"Just so we are clear with each other, am I to understand that we are the provisions he intends to take on?"

"I am afraid that is correct, sir. Rak is soliciting support for an attack on this ship with the intent of taking as many of us as he can as meat for the return trip to their home planet. Most in his armada wants to depart for home where they have families to return to but Rak wants to engage us."

The crew on the bridge all looked at each other in bewilderment. At one moment some of the enemy is leaving but the next instant some are preparing to attack.

"Sam, prepare to detonate the first two devices as soon as they are in lethal contact range of Rak's command ship. I want to damage or destroy as much of his ship as possible."

"JP, start loading as many women and children onto the shuttles as possible. We need to be prepared to send them to safety if our attack on the Yardak fleet goes badly. Megan, please go with JP to help load the shuttles and Megan, no special favors to anyone. Let's save the youngest children and a few caretakers who can go with them."

Megan looked at Walker in horror. She moved over to his side and said, "What about Ryan?"

"Megan, no favors to anyone, including me. I don't deserve to command this ship if I demand or even accept special favors. Understand?"

Walker turned his head away from Megan trying to hide the tears welling up in his eyes. He knew he had said what he should have said but he wasn't really all that pleased with having said it.

Sam held up two fingers so that Walker could see them. He mouthed the words "two minutes."

"Prepare to detonate, Sam."

Sam was leaning over a large scanner indicating the proximity of the two explosive devices to Rak's command ship.

"Fifteen seconds," said Sam so that Walker could hear him.

Walker stood beside him and peered at the screen. "Now," he said to Sam. "Fire."

Sixty seconds later Anya looked over to Walker and said, "My father tells me that Rak's ship has sustained significant damage to the forward and the aft areas. Propulsion capability has been totally destroyed."

General Walker turned toward Sam, shook his hand and thanked him, "Great work Sam. I believe you have saved us from a very unpleasant ending. I'm hoping they will all turn around and head for home."

Samantha interrupted the celebration and said, "General, there is a subspace message from Rak's command ship to you. We can beam the transmission through Anya's father's universal translator so you will be able to communicate with him. Are you ready for this?"

"I am speaking to the commander of the ship that has crippled my ship's propulsion capability. To the soldiers of Yardak, dying in battle is an act of bravery but defeat is the worst possible outcome for a commander because defeat shows weakness."

Captain Walker interrupted Rak and said, "Commander Rak, all we were doing was trying to protect ourselves from attack by your forces. My action against your forces was self-defensive, not a preemptive attack."

"All that matters, sir, is that we have been shamed and have lost our honor in battle. For the shame we have brought upon our people, we will be left to die and our families will be put to death on our home planet by the returning Yardak. There is only one way that we can save our families from this fate."

General Walker already knew what Rak was asking. He was asking for a coup de gras. Walker said, "Commander, I cannot open fire on a defenseless vessel."

"Commander..."

Walker interrupted him and said, "My name is General Seth Walker."

"General Walker, unless you can provide us with a warrior's death, we will float in this piece of space junk, littered with injured troops who will die shortly as the remaining systems in the ship fail. What is worse, we will all die knowing that the returning members of our armada will be bound to carry out their grim duty and execute our families in order to rid our race of the disgrace we have caused. If it helps you to know this, you and your crew would have become food for us on our return voyage if we had captured you."

The General broke the communication with Rak and said, "Samantha, scan Rak's ship for projectiles and get me an ETA on the time to collision of our shuttle with what is left of Rak's ship. I don't trust him."

"Sir, two small projectiles have just been launched from Rak's ship in our direction. I will initiate evasive maneuvers immediately. Also, Sam just informed me that Rak's ship will be in the kill zone from the blast of the shuttle in two minutes."

Samantha said, "I think Rak was trying to appear to be continuing the battle in order to save his reputation as well as the lives of his crew's families."

"He's a shrewd one, this Rak," said Walker. "He wants those members of his armada who hold his crew's families lives in their hands to know that he was fighting till the end which is coming in about fifteen seconds. I hope what he is providing is enough of an offensive show of force to spare his crew's families."

"Sam, prepare to detonate the device on the shuttle."

"Copy that, General."

"Detonate."

"The device has been detonated," reported Sam. He turned to look at the view screen and said, "The ship has been vaporized."

"Now, Samantha, let's be sure to get out of the way of those projectiles. They will be closing in on us in less than an hour."

"General, we will be well out of the way by then. Also, to close the log on this one, the entire Yardak fleet has either been destroyed or has turned and is headed for home to attempt a rescue of their fellow citizens."

In a melancholy tone, General Walker turned to Samantha and said, "I'm sorry about Rak. He didn't have to die. But if he hadn't, his crew's families would have. His sacrifice was a difficult choice but an honorable one. In my view, he was a noble warrior and he has my respect."

They both seemed to be staring at the floor, deep in their own private thoughts, until Walker was suddenly jolted back to matters at hand and said, "Make sure JP doesn't launch those shuttles. It seems we will all be going to Lordune together."

CHAPTER 21

After JP and Megan helped the women and children disembark from the shuttles they walked them back to the nursery. Megan smiled and winked at little Ryan. He recognized her as a friend and smiled back. After that, Megan excused herself, saying she had an errand to run.

A few moments later, Megan opened the door to the cell block where the four protesters were being held. As soon as she looked inside, the ringleader, Dax, recognized her and said in a sarcastic voice, "Look who's here, Mrs. Walker, our old boss from back in the day. I thought I saw you with your ex at the meeting before he sucker-punched me."

Megan looked at the prisoners in their black and white striped prisoner jumpsuits. She scrutinized her former associates with disdain. "Why them? Why now," she thought to herself, "These guys were always bad news. Now they are worse news."

Megan stood in front of the cell door and said, "I was hoping that you had been left on Elon to burn to death. How did you wind up on the prison ship?"

Dax, said, "We guessed that Valerion thought people with our unique talents might be useful to him some day. We've always been good at turning a normal group of people into an unruly mob that would do whatever we wanted them to."

She replied, "What a talent. By the way, I thought there were five of you dirtballs, not just four."

"You better be nice to us. We have plans for you and this ship. Oh, you asked about the fifth one of us. He is behind you now."

She turned to look behind her and all she saw was a fist to the face. The lights went out for Megan as she dropped to the floor.

*****

With the threat of the Yardak behind them, General Walker closed his eyes and let out a deep sigh of relief. While he and the senior team were savoring the freedom from the threat of imminent destruction, he received a call over the ship's intercom from Dax, "General Walker, we are having a reunion in the nursery. We are here with your ex-wife. We convinced her to give us her key to the armory and let me tell you we are now rather well armed."

Walker looked at JP and mouthed, "What's he talking about?"

Dax said, "General, we want to make a trade with you. We'd will trade the kids here in the nursery for control of the ship."

"What do you intend to gain from doing this?" asked Walker quite perplexed. "We are just about to be reunited with the rest of the resistance and we have a good lead on the whereabouts of a good planet to settle on as our new home. What more could you want?"

"No, General. That is your plan. What we want is to recover this ship for Valerion and return it to him. We figure he would be really grateful to see us and get his ship back with all you fine folks on it."

Walker was stunned. He turned to Anya and said, "Contact my brother. Have him send Li Kang and her squad over here in a shuttle."

"I communicated directly to Li," said Anya. "She will be in the flight bay in ninety minutes."

After several minutes of communication silence, Dax said, "I'm waiting, General. You need to talk to me before we start having target practice with these fine weapons."

Before Walker responded to Dax, he took the ship's intercom and broadcast a message to everyone on the ship: "This is General Walker. I want to let you know that the concern about the Yardak is now over. They are returning to their home planet and none of us will be harmed. For now, we are all safe from them. But that brings me to a new issue. Several armed men who once worked for Valerion have entered the nursery and have taken your children hostage. They are demanding that I turn over control of the ship to them. Their intent is to return the ship and everyone on it to Valerion. I am certain you understand what that will mean to all of us. Most of you will return to a lifetime of slavery instead of freedom. As you know, freedom for us is only twenty-four hours away. I have brought the ship to All Stop and have sent the captain and her flight crew off the ship to Lordune in a shuttle. For your safety, I must suggest that those of you with children in the nursery not go down to confront these men as they are obviously unstable."

The red light on the hand set of the communication device lit up like it was on fire. "You bastard," screamed Dax. "Unstable? Let me tell you what is going to happen. You will come down here and we will all take the elevator back to the bridge. Once we get there, we will release the kids and you and your ex-wife will join us on the bridge while you recall the flight crew. Once they get back on this ship, we will locate Valerion and set a course straight for him."

"No, Dax. That is not what is going to happen. You and your associates will take the elevator to the bridge with or without my ex-wife. I don't really care what you do with her. When you reach the bridge, I will unlock the elevator door and you will have me as your hostage. But you will leave all the children and the other adults in the nursery."

"Having you and your ex-wife as hostages plus control of the bridge is what we want. We will be there in ten minutes. Be ready for us."

"I'll be waiting," said Walker.

As soon as the communication with Dax ended, Walker turned to Anya and asked her to get in touch with Li and tell her that when they arrive, they will pretend to be the returning flight crew. Tell them they will be searched by the hostage takers so be prepared for that.

"JP, take Samantha and everyone else on the bridge to a safe place to hide. I believe when Li and her crew get here, the hostage situation should be resolved very quickly. Li is an apex predator and thrives on encounters like this."

*****

One of Dax's henchmen, Little John, said, "Dax, I don't see your plan working like we hoped. Walker seems to be one step ahead of us all the time. Do you really think he cares if we shoot his ex-wife? I mean, she is his ex-wife."

"Listen, Little John, Walker just outsmarted himself. When we go to the bridge, I'm going to leave you and your brother down here. With you two here, he won't dare give us any problems. I think I'll leave his old lady down here too. She's still unconscious since your brother slugged her in the face."

Feeling smug like he had devised the perfect plan, Dax looked over his shoulder proudly and said to the other two, "Let's go take over our new ship and set a course back to Valerion."

On the trip up the elevator to the bridge, one of his two accomplices said, "Do you really believe that Valerion will welcome us back instead of having us just disappear?"

Dax replied, "Valerion values loyalty more than anything. Besides that, he hates Walker and will be thrilled to see him return undamaged. We will get a hero's welcome. No doubt."

*****

Dax strode out of the open elevator door with Megan's sidearm in his hand. In his mind, he was a shrewd operator who had won a staggering victory over the great, formerly omnipotent General Walker. Walker was standing next to the main control panel on the bridge. The rabble rouser was taller than Walker but Walker was built like an athlete and Dax looked like a twig. He really wanted to kill Walker for humiliating him when they first met but he was smart enough to know that if anyone had the keys to getting him and his party back to Valerion, it was Walker.

"Where's the crew?" demanded Dax.

"I told you I had sent them away on a shuttle?"

"Where is my ex-wife? Did one of you big, strong bruisers beat the little lady so badly she can't make the trip up here?"

"She was shaken up when we were trying to disarm her."

"Who hit her? I want his name."

"You aren't making the rules here, Walker. I make the rules and I want the flight crew back here now. We've got places to go."

Walker walked toward his opponent who had greatly overestimated his dominance over the General. As Walker approached the professional mouthpiece, Dax raised his weapon and pointed it at him. Walker closed the distance between himself until the barrel of his ex-wife's side arm until it was just inches from his chest.

In Walker's mind, Dax was all talk. He was a big mouth who incited others to action while seldom taking any himself. The General could see the weapon shaking in the bully's clammy hand.

"Look, Dax, I'm guessing there isn't one functioning brain cell among the five of you. If you want to believe that you have the upper hand, I'll play that game with you. But know this, this ship goes nowhere until I see my ex-wife."

"Well, General, I am the one with the weapon and with the hostages. I'd say that makes me the big man in charge. Right?"

"No, dumbass. If you shoot me, what do you think you are going to do? None of you can operate a star ship like this, you can't operate the radio, you can't find Valerion, in fact, you can't do anything except wave that pistol around. Now go get Ms. Murray and be quick about it. Also, I want to know the name of the coward who slugged her from behind."

"How'd you know she was slugged from behind?"

"You just admitted it, you dunce," said Walker.

Walker's brain was bubbling with questions, "Was she badly hurt or was she dead? What about the children? Was Li going to arrive before Dax lost his last little bit of self-control and started shooting?"

Aside from those potentially explosive uncertainties, to Walker the situation possessed an almost comical quality. Dax and his men were so inept at hostage taking as to be entertaining. Until the captain returned to the bridge, Walker was more in control of the situation than Dax.

The General choreographed several scenarios for taking the weapon away from Dax and shooting him and possibly one of the other two. The third one would be more of a challenge. Then there was the matter of the other two in the nursery.

Dax motioned for the shorter of his two henchmen to come over to where he was standing so they could strategize. He spoke loudly enough for Walker to hear what he said, "Go to the nursery and bring Walker's ex-wife back with you. Then, tell Little John and Jordy to get ready to start shooting kids if he doesn't get the flight crew back here in a hurry."

Adrenaline shot through Walker's body as he knew that now was to be his best chance to take these two fanatics out and reclaim the bridge. As soon as fanatic number one entered the elevator, Walker said in a loud and defiant manner, "You don't think having my ex-wife up here will provide you any leverage with me, do you?"

Dax took the bait and walked up to Walker and leveled the weapon at the general's forehead.

"Showtime," thought Walker as he coiled his reflexes, ready to strike.

In less than a second Walker grabbed the weapon with his left hand and simultaneously rammed the heel of his right hand into the wrist of Dax's gun hand. Dax's grip on the pistol was jarred loose and Walker twisted the weapon out of his hand dislocating his opponent's trigger finger. Within two seconds Walker was pointing the weapon at Dax's forehead.

While Dax was howling about his finger, the other thug turned in Walker's direction to fire. Walker fired before he had gotten set to shoot and put a blue pulse through his chest.

Walker looked his whimpering adversary in the face and said, "I should shoot you for the problems you have caused. Now sit down on that bench while I answer this incoming communication."

The voice on the communicator said, "General, is that you? This is Kang. We have landed and I am on my way to the bridge. What is your situation and how can we help?"

While Walker and Kang were speaking, Dax's left hand, the one with no broken fingers, was making its way to his right boot which held a concealed firearm. As he was about to raise his pant leg and retrieve the firearm, Walker turned his gaze toward the assailant causing Dax to move his hand away from his boot casually as if he was stretching.

The elevator door opened and Walker turned to see if it was friend or foe. He let out a sigh of relief as Li Kang bolted out of the door to assess the situation for herself. "What choo got here, General?" she asked in soldier vernacular. "Looks like a bit of a mess."

"Five of Valerion's riot squad were trying to steal the ship that we liberated from Valerion. This one's alive and that one's not. This whimpering mess on the floor is the leader and there are three more down in the nursery that we have to take care of. All three are armed."

Li was surveying the man on the floor as the elevator door closed. She noticed that Dax was rubbing his right leg with his left hand. Right leg – left hand, something seemed wrong. "By the way, General, did you have time to search this dirt bag? I'm anxious to see if there is anything in his right boot. He keeps fiddling with it like he is digging for buried treasure."

Li walked up to Dax with her sidearm in her hand. She scowled at him and said, "I don't have much time before your buddies arrive here on the bridge so I am only going to ask you this only once. Do you have a weapon in your boot?" As short as she was, she was a menacing presence. She peered at him through eye slits that make her look like a snake.

Dax looked at the weapon with his eyes wide open and said, "No way, mam."

"I notice that you are sweating. Is there some reason that you are nervous?"

"The General broke my trigger finger and now you are threatening to shoot me for having some imaginary pistol in my boot. Who wouldn't be sweating?"

"I didn't say pistol. You are the one who said pistol."

She leveled her pistol at his crotch and said, "You will spend the rest of your days as a unic if I find a weapon on you. Now kick your right boot off with your left foot. Keep your hands where I can see them."

Dax gave in, "Alright, alright, there is a pistol in my right boot. Please don't shoot me," he pleaded.

Li quickly stepped behind him and bound his hands behind his back. She said, "You would have killed me or the General if you could have. The way I look at it, you are on a death sentence that is only one more screw up away. Now kick off your right boot."

She retrieved the fire arm and snarled at him, "You sniveling weasel. You don't know how bad I want to end your worthless life. I'm really afraid I'm going to have nightmares if I don't shoot you."

The General whispered, "Pssssst, the elevator sounds like it is on the way. Let's turn off the lights and put him into a corner on the floor. Keep him out of the way so he can't be seen when the door opens. There should only be one of Dax's men and he will have Megan with him."

"What about your ex-wife," asked Li as she stepped into the shadows in front of Dax?

"Let's both try not to shoot her," said the General with his old concerns about her loyalty beginning to resurface. He headed to the master light switch and darkened the room.

The metallic elevator door opened spilling light into the darkened bridge. Megan and her captor, the one known as Little John, stood at the opening, framed in light. She was in front of him.

Li pushed her pistol into Dax's solar plexus and whispered, "Tell him to come into the bridge and turn on the lights or I will blow a hole through your chest."

The pain was intense as Li forced the barrel of her weapon into his chest and Dax had no doubt the violent woman standing over him would kill him. He shouted out, "Get in here and turn on the lights. I'm wounded."

The Little John's self-preservation instincts were heightened as he stepped into the darkness. He couldn't see Dax and was beginning to suspect that all was just not right. His grip on Megan's belt tightened as did the grip on his side arm. Droplets of nervous sweat were forming on his forehead and running down his face through his scraggly brown beard.

Li had changed the position of her pistol from his chest to his neck. She told him what to say and he said, "The General is dead and I have been wounded. Get out here and give me a hand."

Hearing Dax, he pushed Megan forward into the part of the bridge that was illuminated by the elevator light and followed her slowly. A hand reached out from the blackness and grabbed Megan, pulling her in.

Little John, awash in elevator light, was indeed feeling quite alone and quite exposed. He whimpered, "Dax, where are you? I cannot see a thing."

Dax, no longer feeling the pressure of Li's sidearm on his neck, summoned the nerve to shout to Little John, "Shoot her. She is standing next to me. Shoot, shoot, shoot."

Little John, not being able to see his leader but also not wanting to disobey, began to fire in the direction of Dax's voice. He fired three times hoping to hit someone other than his boss. One second later a blue streak pulsed out of the darkness and went through his chest. He dropped like a bag of rocks.

"Li, are you alright?" shouted the General.

"I'm fine but I'm not so sure about Dax."

The General turned the lights on. In the corner near the elevator door was Dax who had been shot by Little John. Standing six feet away was Li Kang with a smoldering burn hole next to her head. Little John had missed her by inches before she fired at him.

To punctuate the silence, the elevator doors closed and the elevator descended.

The three survivors of the attempted takeover of the bridge exchanged mystified glances.

Megan said, "It must be the two down in the nursery wondering what is happening here on the bridge."

When the elevator returned to the bridge and the doors opened, the two remaining members of Dax's crew were standing in the doorway, back-to-back, with their hands secured behind them. A voice from behind them shouted, "This is JP. I would be grateful if you didn't shoot."

"Come on out of there, JP. Looks like I need to thank you one more time," shouted the General.

JP shoved the two out of the elevator and he followed them, smiling.

Two of us were keeping an eye on the goings on in the nursery with the security cameras in the ceiling. He said, "When we saw an opportunity, we rushed them and took them down."

"We? Who else was with you, JP?" asked Walker.

"I got a lot of help from Jason Stockton. Seems to be a friend of Lt. Kang," said JP with an *I Know a Secret* kind of smile. After that introduction, Stockton stepped out of the elevator cab and briefly acknowledged General Walker before scanning the room. His gaze locked onto Li's. Their hearts started pounding a bit faster as soon as they saw each other.

Just the mention of Jason's name made Li check her watch to see how much longer before her shift ended. Jason had come with her on the shuttle from Lordune but upon arrival they parted ways. Jason's coming with JP told Li more than he could have with words.

CHAPTER 22

Valerion avoided personal relationships with everyone as if they all had the plague. You could easily say, he had an aversion to personal relationships. Of course, he tolerated the pandering of sycophants but he took their blabbering as mere background noise and nothing of any importance. For a moment, however, his new second in command, now Chancellor Nardin, was as close to a confidant as anyone by virtue of his exposing the plot of the High Council against him. Still, Valerion had no interest in his companionship.

Several days after being elevated to his new position, Chancellor Nardin, requested an audience with Valerion. He asked, as respectfully as possible, "How long before the armada will be arriving at our new home planet?"

Valerion kept the destination, which in his mind had been wrenched from the memory of the little alien named Anya, a closely guarded secret from everyone except the senior flight crew. Without bothering to look up at the Chancellor, Valerion said, "Why do you ask, Chancellor Nardin?"

"Excellency," he replied guardedly, already wishing he had not asked the question, "The people in the armada are looking to me for answers about when we will arrive at our new home planet."

Valerion slowly raised his head and said, with an ominous stare, "I'll answer your question but you must keep what I am about to tell you extremely confidential." Valerion said, "When we started out on this expedition from Elon, we had more than one thousand workers and craftsmen on the prison transport. Thanks to our friend Walker," he said with a nasty sneer, "those workers are no longer available to us. Nevertheless, when we land, someone will have to do the physical, heavy work and it is not going to be me."

Having no difficulty grasping the seriousness of what Valerion was telling him, Nardin said, "I understand, sir. I also hope it isn't me either."

Without alleviating his underling's anxiety with the courtesy of a response, Valerion continued, "We will be approaching our new home in about three months. Before we land, we will need to determine which of our passengers may be forced to become workers and who will survive as part of the privileged class. Unless we can find a ready source of essentially slave labor, we will be forced to convert many of our own passengers to a laborer status."

Nardin said, "Sir, obviously this is going to upset a lot of people."

Valerion looked at Nardin with half a smile and said, "They will be more than upset. They will be near revolution. However, if we are going to survive as a people, there will need to be workers. Unless we are fortunate enough to find a ready pool of native inhabitants on our new home planet, we must use those who came with us."

"My Lord, I understand but if we must force our own supporters to become common workers, they will be calling for our heads."

"Isn't it fortunate that we have all the soldiers and all the weapons? They have no choice except to comply," said Valerion, the gamesman, with a widening grin.

"Now, my dear Chancellor, lest you think I have not thought this scheme, as you call it, thru, let me tell you that at this very moment, several space cruisers with most of our military troops are preparing to land on our new home in order to get an early assessment of conditions on the ground."

"Do you have any early indications of inhabitants on the planet's surface?" asked Nardin with an anxious look on his face. His eyes were as wide as saucers.

"As a matter of a fact, there is evidence of life on the planet, as you might expect for a planet with the physical gifts that this one has. The question remains, however, as to how useful its inhabitants will be."

"Useful? I should think that we might want to cooperate with them and join them for our mutual benefit."

"If you remember, my dear Chancellor, we did not cooperate with anyone on Elon. We dominate. They either joined us or we destroyed them. Recall?"

"I recall decades of death and destruction all to control a dying planet."

"You disappoint me, Nardin. Elon was only the first phase of my plan. The final phase is to establish a dominant position on a vibrant planet and use that planet's occupants to help us create our new world. It is my sincere expectation that the original occupants of this planet will constitute our workforce to help us build a thriving, new world."

He knew the others in the High Council hated Nardin for betraying them. At the same time, Valerion knew he couldn't trust Nardin any more than the High Council did. He considered including Nardin in his first status update with the portion of the fleet that was circling their new home but decided against it. He thought, "If there is anything except excellent news, the last thing I need is a turncoat like Nardin with that information which could be used to undermine my position."

Chapter 23

Sorrengia – Valerion's would-be Elon

In one of his few rare moments between emergencies, the General searched the ship for Anya. He wanted her to clarify his understanding of what kind of conditions Valerion would encounter when he lands on the planet that Anya "revealed" to him when he was "torturing" her.

"That is an interesting question, General. Why so curious?" asked Anya as her self-defense reflexes became energized.

"I just want you to make me feel certain that Valerion will never again be a threat to The People or, for that matter, anyone else. I don't know what to say, Anya, but I want to know what kind of world he is going to encounter when he lands on the planet you directed him to."

"No problem, General. Why not find a comfortable place to sit. This will take a while to explain because Valerion is headed to a complex environment."

"Mind if I ask JP to join us? He is my backup in case something happens to me."

"It will be good to have him with us. As you may remember, he and I have been friends for quite some time. Let us have him join us in the lounge on level 4."

"The planet they were directed to is called Sorrengia. It is, or was, inhabited by a cerebral race of peaceful beings who had large, hairless heads and very thin arms and legs. For centuries, the Sorrengians enjoyed peace and prosperity because of their advances in science, medicine, and technology."

JP said, "It seems to me that Valerion and his people would have no problem dominating a planet populated by peaceful scientists."

"Let me go on," she said. "You will understand why I sent them to Sorrengia when I finish the story. There was one fatal flaw affecting the Sorrengians and this shortcoming was of their own making. That one issue changed this once serene panacea into something quite different – much more sinister."

"Tell us, Anya. We are all ears," said the General.

Anya looked with a wrinkled brow at Walker, not being familiar with the term, "We were all ears."

JP realized her confusion and quickly clarified the meaning of the slang phrase. "What the general means is that we are anxious to hear the rest of the story."

Relieved and slightly embarrassed, Anya smiled sheepishly and continued, "With their scientific advances, the Sorrengians had cured most known diseases and, as a result, life expectancies grew dramatically longer. After disease was no longer a health risk, the technical hierarchy directed their scientific efforts to permanently enhancing the bodies of the Sorrengians. Over time, if a body part wore out, broke down, or became diseased, the defective part was simply replaced with a mechanical replica. As decades passed, a growing number of Sorrengians were increasingly more mechanical than biological."

Walker said, "You mean they were converting themselves into cyborgs. Right?"

"That was not the original intent. The impetus for the trend to create perfect, mechanical bodies out of living beings initially came from the well-meaning technical hierarchy, referred to as The Commission. The majority of the Sorrengians were completely unaware of the dramatic changes planned by The Commission. They were simply living their lives and pursuing their own passions while enjoying the benefits of the decline of life-threatening diseases. The scientific cult did what creative geniuses do with unlimited resources but no critical oversight: they delved into socially questionable areas of scientific endeavor that most of the population would probably not want explored."

The General observed, "One problem I have with this process of replacing original-issue biological body parts with manufactured, mechanical parts is that sooner or later the mechanized person will no longer possess those things what made the person who he was. My guess is that The Commission could not replace the person's personality with a mechanical personality."

"General," Anya said putting her hands up to signal him to stop leaping to conclusions, "you are correct but that is not the most significant part of the issue. Let me continue."

"Sorry, Anya. I just get worried when I conjure up the image of Valerion getting his hands on an army of mechanical, programmable soldiers."

He and JP shared a concerned glance. Both could visualize an army of robots controlled by Valerion. They both could imagine an ending to this story that had a much more negative implication for The People than they initially thought.

Anya continued, "One of the final steps in The Commission's conversion of organic beings into increasingly more mechanical beings was a complete replacement of the internal organs. With these enhancements, the new mechanized citizens no longer required food to eat or air to breathe."

"What do you mean they no longer breathed air or ate food?" said Walker, who did not see this coming.

"Think back to your biology classes in early school. You learned that food is eaten to provide energy to our bodies and air is breathed to deliver oxygen to our cells so the cells can convert food into energy."

The two soldiers' mouths were agape in stunned disbelief until the General said, "If they don't eat food or breathe air, what did they do for energy?"

"The cyborgs, as well as the Central Computer itself, were designed to be powered by dicatna crystals found in abundance on their home planet. These glowing crystals were the fuel that powered fusion cells to produce energy. The crystals were found deep inside mines in the hills of Sorrengia. With the newer technology and access to an abundant power source, several thousand biologics were transitioned from flesh and bone to machine beings, or cyborgs," she said.

"Anya," JP said, "This conversion process was a gigantic societal leap that The Commission took without consulting the Sorrengians. How could this happen?"

"You are right, JP. The Sorrengians were so busy enjoying their hedonistic lives that they failed to pay attention to the work going on in the scientific community. Their inability to monitor or control the activities of The Commission was the fatal flaw that I mentioned earlier."

"But Anya," said the General, "how did The Commission get away with such a perversion of their original intent to improve the health of the populace?"

"The Commission's shift in attitude occurred in two ways. First, it was done in secret and second it was done slowly, you might say in secret. About thirty-five years ago, The Commission came under the control of an ambitious but brilliant scientist named Gant. He realized the potential of completely mechanical beings and altered the computer's primary directive into creating enhanced units which could be used for extraterrestrial exploration and conquest. Space is an environment where there is no food and there is no oxygen. From the standpoint of the megalomaniacal Doctor Gant, the shift made perfect sense."

"Didn't the people have anything to say about their neighbors disappearing only to return to their former neighborhoods as shiny, metal robots?" asked JP whimsically.

"Like I said earlier, the intent of the original technical elite was not to create an army of fierce looking cyborgs. Initially the purpose was only to extend and enhance the lives of the Sorrengians. Considerable care was taken to make the converted models look as much like the original Sorrengians as possible. The major difference in physical appearance was that the more mechanical a Sorrengian became, the heavier his arms and legs to support the additional weight of their new internal equipment."

"Okay," JP said, "but you certainly could tell a cyborg from a biologic. Right?"

"Yes, anyone could tell when the process had been completed. The converted citizens were heavier and bulkier than the biologics. But they were also faster, stronger, and smarter. As the number of cyborgs grew, there arose increasingly noisy protests amongst the population who were stunned when faced with a wave of superior bodies that had been mechanically enhanced. The Sorrengians slowly realized they were no longer at the top of the food chain on Sorrengia."

"I understand the androids were stronger because of the bionic limbs, but why smarter?" asked Walker.

"The conversion process was only finally complete when the enhanced models had received a computer implanted in their skulls," said Anya. "In other words...."

The General finished her sentence, "In other words, their brains were replaced with an advanced computer node networked to the Central Computer."

"Yes," she said. "That was bad but there's still more."

"Let me guess," said the General. "This is the point in time where Gant and perhaps others in The Commission become increasingly more paranoid when faced with popular opposition to the drastic changes they had been making to their own people. The good of the people on Sorrengia became increasingly insignificant to the Commission as their own selfish plans, which was exactly the path that Valerion took on Elon, became the driving force to the Commission. Gant turned into a monster and began creating changes that brought ruin to his people."

"That is correct," said Anya. "Gant turned into another Valerion and both were consumed by the lust for power."

Knowing they had seen a scenario like this played out before on Elon with Valerion, Walker and JP leaned forward in their chairs and buried their heads in their hands in dejection.

"It's bad enough to have gone through this on Elon but to know that the Sorrengians had to experience the same thing is totally miserable," said JP.

Anya continued, "In order to protect their mechanical science project from being slowed or halted by an increasingly hostile public, Gant made several drastic adjustments to the control program of the Central

Computer. This code change caused an immediate transition within the Central Computer to the notion that the biologics (the unconverted Sorrengians) were not just a potential threat but a dangerous threat. Any biologic that protested too loudly or violently was considered an enemy of the state and immediately sanctioned (eliminated or jailed). The cyborgs began rounding up the populace and forcing them into reconditioning camps. Many were killed mercilessly."

"*Originally, The Commission was the only entity with access to the Central Computer and the Central Computer controlled the cyborgs.* However, when it became clear that the Sorrengians were on the verge of insurrection, Gant made another fatal mistake. Like the paranoid sociopath that he was, he restricted access to the computer to everyone except himself by installing a palm reading security device that recognized only his right palm."

"I feel like we have all heard this story before. Where is the happy ending?" asked Walker.

"From hindsight, you could see it coming like a slow-motion collision of an asteroid and a planet. When the unenhanced population finally became aware of the details of what had happened to thousands of their countrymen, they erupted into revolution. It was a civil war of the physically hapless biologics against the computer and their former countrymen, the computer's cyborg army."

"How could a gentle race like the Sorrengians hope to defeat such an enemy?" asked Walker.

"The Sorrengians knew they had to defeat the cyborgs or they would all die. The popular leader of the biologics, a clever programmer named Luk, devised a dramatic plan consisting of two bold moves. Luk realized that the entire cyborg existence had two fatal vulnerabilities. The first was that the Central Computer and its cyborg minions were completely dependent on dicatna crystals. The first part of his overall strategy was to go to the mines and create an explosion of such magnitude that it would bring down the entire top half of the mountain onto the mines. That would seal the mines shut for years."

"And the second part?" said JP eagerly.

"Luk knew that if they could destroy the crystals and deprive the computers of their energy source, the machines would all run out of power within two or three weeks. However, even if they were successful in destroying the crystals the cyborgs were still fully capable of wiping out all Sorrengians on the planet while they still had energy. The second part of Luk's strategy was to capture the Central Computer and attempt to reprogram it. The reprogramming would allow the biologics to survive and then they would neutralize The Commission."

He also realized the Sorrengians were physically incapable of climbing the steep mountains to the mines or carrying enough explosives to do the job. For this portion of the plan, he solicited the help of several hundred partially enhanced biologics and recruited them into the service of their people. They had the arms and legs of a cyborg but not the computer implant.

Walker asked, "Why would partially enhanced robots turn against Gant and his all-cyborg army?"

The answer to this question personally pained Anya. Her gaze turned down as she spoke in monotone. She said, "The process of finally taking away the last of a Sorrengian's biological functions was all in a day's work for the technical elite. It was not so easy for the patient who would finally become little more than a node in the computer's network. As the unenhanced biologics distaste for the enhancement process began to grow, even though complete enhancement meant a form of immortality, Gant and The Commission realized that the remaining partially enhanced cyborgs could become a liability. They were beginning to resist being turned into cyborgs en masse."

JP and Walker were mesmerized with the drama unfolded by Anya. "Let's continue with the story, Anya. Like you said earlier, this sad fall of their entire civilization was primarily of their own doing," said Walker. "The Sorrengians failed to keep a watchful eye on the creative elements of their society."

The two-pronged plan involved attacking the Central Computer simultaneously with blowing up the mines. One thing Luk and his small band could not afford was to be discovered by Gant who would have stopped them with ease.

As Luk and his small squad of partially enhanced cyborgs, who were armed with the same pulsar weapons implanted inside Gant's cyborgs, approached the Central Computer building, Luk gave the electronic signal to blow the mines. The noise from the blast was deafening even from miles away.

As Luk turned his head to watch the plume of smoke pour out of the mountain, he knew that life on his planet would never be the same. He only hoped that he could get to the computer and reprogram it for the good of his people.

Gant never foresaw the possibility of an armed intrusion by the placid Sorrengians. He was totally caught off guard when Luk and his band blew the doors off the computer building and rushed toward the main computer terminal. The terminal itself was in a small room surrounded by hardened glass to protect it from unauthorized entry. Gant stood wide-eyed inside the room as the intruders surged toward him.

When Gant saw the Sorrengian leading the partially enhanced biologics, he was stunned by the realization that his resent programming contained one fatal omission. He had *not* marked the partially enhanced biologics for destruction along with the Sorrengians. He never foresaw that the partially enhanced cyborgs would turn on him. He desperately pounded the keyboard and entered one final instruction, "Destroy all biologics, whether partially enhanced or not enhanced."

At this point two critical events occurred. First was that the Central Computer sensed the explosion immediately with its buried seismic sensors. The computer was programmed to interpret such a blast as a potential threat and took immediate precautions to protect itself. The computer called all available cyborgs to come and defend the Central Computer from whatever threat might be associated with the shockwave.

Within minutes, hundreds of cyborgs began to converge on the computer building.

Luk turned and cried out to his small band, which was about to be overrun by the cyborgs, "Hold them off as long as you can. I will try to get inside the room and reprogram the computer."

Within two or three minutes, Gant's cyborgs had destroyed Luk's followers. Luk was wounded several times before he died with his bony hand on the outside handle to the control room door.

Gant's normally expressionless face lit up in ghoulish delight as he savored the rebel force being overrun. As soon as the last of Luk's followers was dispatched, he bolted out of the control room to delight in his one-sided victory firsthand. He was excited to savor the sweetness of his triumph.

What he did not see coming, however, was one cyborg raising his weapon and yelling, "Biologic." All the others in the room raised their weapons and said in unison with their metallic voices, "Biologic." Gant was blasted into atoms by over one hundred of his robots who were dutifully following his final instruction to the computer.

Within two months, the cyborgs had relentlessly hunted down and decimated all the Sorrengians including what remained of The Commission. All that was left on Sorrengia was several thousand robots whose power supplies were almost exhausted.

Walker said, "When Valerion and his people arrive on Sorrengia, how much life will be left in the batteries?"

"I anticipate that all the cyborgs will have exhausted their batteries by the time of Valerion's arrival," she replied with a smile. "It will be a very still and lifeless world."

"This is both a sad and amazing story, Anya, but I have to ask if there is any way for Valerion to reenergize the robots?"

"General, there are two factors that argue against Valerion having any success on Sorrengia. The first is that, in the unlikely event Valerion can power up the robots with something other than dicatna crystals, the first command the robots will follow is the last command they received from the Central Computer: to kill the new biologics, the Elonese. The second factor is that the Central Computer is permanently locked because of Gant's placing the palm reading security device as the final key to unlocking access to the computer. No part of Gant exists any longer."

"Does that sound secure enough, general?"

"I'd hate to make an enemy out of you, young lady," said JP with a smile.

"I don't think you have to worry about that, JP," she said as their eyes locked in a glance that left JP with exploding emotions that he had not felt in many years.

Walker said, "I feel unspeakably sad that a race as gentle and advanced as the Sorrengians was annihilated just because of the malignant hunger for power of a few individuals."

"Believe me, General, I have seen this destructive hunger infect beings throughout the Universe. One of the prime directives of The Builders is to curb the ruinous lust for power and control when we find it."

Despite that, lurking in the back of Anya's mind was the gnawing concern that even if the robots were out of the equation entirely, Valerion could still be a menace to all those remaining of the people of Elon. What could she do? What should she do?"

Anya arose slowly from her chair and stretched out her tiny arms. She was worried about the situation that was about to unfold on Sorrengia but she had no one to share her concerns with. She said, "General, with your permission, I think I will go back to my room and take a rest."

"We all probably need some down time. Even hearing this story takes a lot out of you."

The General and his friend, JP, watched Anya as she made her way to the door. Walker turned his head toward JP and said, "I get the feeling that something is bothering our little friend. I need to feel as confident as she tried to appear concerning the robots on Sorrengia. Gant was bad but Valerion with those robots could be a disaster for us."

JP replied, "I got the same vibe of concern from her."

"I know you two are close," said the General. "Do you think you could pay her a visit? I get the feeling that she would appreciate someone to talk with. As you and I have both observed, she is obviously different from any woman I have ever known. She might be impressed if you told her you were concerned about her feelings."

"I gotta be honest with you, sir," he said with a smile, "I was thinking seriously about doing that anyway."

CHAPTER 24

Sorrengia - The Planet of the Dead

Valerion had not felt this vulnerable in many years. The greatest source of his unease was that most of his armed forces was far away with Commander Ludorn preparing to assert domination over their new planet. His army and his chief of internal security, Zadorn, were his main sources of control. But now he was left with Zadorn, Ludorn's younger brother, and a smattering of security forces to keep any unrest at bay until the main force of his army returned.

In his paranoid mind, he was under immense pressure to deliver a habitable planet for his "friends and supporters" in the armada. More than his prestige was at stake. His failure to stop Walker, whose flamboyant escape from the armada together with over one thousand would-be workers, stung Valerion like a wound that would not heal. He needed this planet to be all that anyone could want in a new home world.

Privately, Valerion was deeply concerned for his prospects for survival if he failed again. He began to liken the High Council to a group of hungry vultures watching as their wounded prey struggled to resist the sweet embrace of death.

Valerion contacted Commander Ludorn, "Commander, I want you to describe the situation you observe on the surface of the planet."

"Of course, Mr. President. We have scanned the surface and have established a geostationary orbit above the primary grouping of buildings on the planet. To put it simply, the surface is eerily quiet. There is no movement except for plants moving in the wind and numerous packs of wolves scavenging the area."

Valerion blurted out, "You mean there are buildings but you have seen no one to occupy them? That makes no sense. Is it possible that the occupants may be hiding?"

"We are thousands of miles above the surface and, while it is not impossible that they have detected us, we have detected no heat signatures from any organic beings on the surface other than small animals. It is very quiet down there, sir. Very still. It seems to me that we are flying over the city of the dead."

"This is ridiculous, Ludorn. Someone built the city. You need to get down to the surface and tell me who built those buildings and where they are."

"Sir, with your permission, I would like to land on the planet and take an expeditionary group to survey the structures. If we encounter problems, I will summon the remainder of our forces for support."

"No, Commander. The situation is urgent. You will land every soldier on the surface and you will survey every structure, every building, and every place where one or more natives could be hiding and report back to me in 24 hours. I need to know who built these structures and if they are a threat. Understand?"

Sensing the subject was not up for debate, Ludorn answered, "Sir, I hear and I obey."

*****

24 hours later:

"Mr. President, I am ready with my report," said Ludorn.

"Continue," said Valerion who could hardly contain himself in his eagerness to hear good news from the planet surface. "I am listening with your brother, Zadorn."

"Mr. President, on the surface of the planet is a scene of considerable carnage. The remains of what seems like many tens of thousands of the former inhabitants of the planet are found within the city and scattered for miles outside the city where they appear to have been fleeing. It seems they have all been killed with advanced pulsar weapons."

"Is there any indication of who killed them?"

"That brings us to another part of the issue. It looks like thousands of the indigenous population have been converted from the same kind of beings who have been killed to mechanical beings or cyborgs. Most cyborgs show no apparent damage and it is most unclear if the robots are dead or if they ceased to function. To answer your question, it appears that the only ones on the planet that could have killed the natives are the mechanical beings."

"Have the medical team do autopsies on the cyborgs as well as the native population. We need to find out what can be learned of the previous occupants of this planet."

"That process is already under way," said Ludorn.

"Ludorn, I also need to know why the cyborgs stopped functioning. If they are simply dead, I need to know that. If they can be reenergized, that would solve a lot of my problems and I need to know that. Robots do not require threats or intimidation," Valerion said with a widening grin as he imagined the benefits of an army of robots at his command.

*****

Anya was sitting quietly in her room with the lights off. She stared blankly out a window at a cluster of stars several billion miles away. She couldn't shake the anguish that leading Valerion to an army of robots, which at one time seemed inert, could prove disastrous for the Elonese as well as The People under Walker's care if Valerion was able to find a suitable power source for them. That concern was a matter she could not share with anyone on the rebel transport. The only one she could share her concerns with was her father.

"Father," she thought, "Please tell me you are monitoring the activities on Sorrengia. The threat of Valerion makes the situation more complex than any of our previous planetary developmental activities."

"My dear daughter, you are correct. His cruel and evil presence makes your efforts most difficult. With or without his control of the androids, it is difficult to imagine an ideal ending to this chapter with Valerion in the picture."

"He is exactly like Gant," thought Ely's daughter.

"That is correct," he replied, having heard her thoughts, "but we can interfere no more. You and I will have some explaining to do about your directing Valerion to Sorrengia instead of a less problematic planet. Our task is to assist civilizations in their development, not to expose them to imminent danger because of your animosity toward their leader. We are Builders, not destroyers."

"It was all I could do to keep myself from sending Valerion's convoy into scanner range of the Yardak because I knew what the Yardak would do to them."

"Anya, always keep those thoughts to yourself and hide them deep within your mind. That kind of thinking would be the end of your service with the Builders."

"Of course, Father."

"Just remember, The Builders are responsible for assisting and developing new, promising civilizations in this universe. There is always the hope that what remains of the Elonese may develop into a civilization for the benefit of all rather than for the benefit of the few."

"Yes, Father."

Anya, who was one of the younger of The Builders, was a veteran of several hundred years of independent operations among developing civilizations in the Universe. Still, she felt a huge burden of responsibility because she alone had directed Valerion to Sorrengia in the hope that the Elonese would thrive on Sorrengia and perhaps overthrow Valerion as their leader. What she had failed to consider was the possibility that Valerion could find a way to reenergize the androids and make them into an almost invincible army. That mistake weighed heavily on little Anya. She could think of no way to correct her mistake.

Little Anya, whose size belied the extent of her psychic power, was conflicted by her allegiance to The Builder's Principle of Neutrality and her desire to seek justice for those murdered on Elon by Valerion and his army. Yet she could no longer interfere directly as the scenario on Sorrengia unfolded. Further overt actions to Valerion's detriment would certainly attract the attention of the Builder's Council. That could permanently threaten her position with the Builders and, by implication, her sister and father could come under the cloud of suspicion.

*****

JP was anxious as he approached the door to her cabin. He wiped his hands on his pants to dry the nervous perspiration. He felt like a schoolboy who finally worked up the nerve to "drop by" and visit the prom queen. As he approached the door and was about to announce himself, the door opened framing Anya, wearing an all-white robe, with an angelic smile. She said, "I'm so glad you are here."

"Come in," she said. "What a nice surprise to see you."

JP was unsure why Anya would be in a room that was pitch black. He said jokingly, "Would you like for me to speak to the chief engineer about fixing the lights in your room?"

"Sorry," she said with a loud laugh. "It helps me relax when I pray with the lights off. Let me turn one or two on for you."

"Thanks very much, I do not want to be a bother. I just came by to ask if you were feeling ill. You seemed distracted earlier."

Anya's head drooped to hide her smile. She thought, "My dear JP, I am immortal and cannot be sick." But then she turned to look at him and said, "Why thank you for your concern, JP. So much has happened lately that I was just reflecting on our amazing journey since we escaped from Valerion's convoy. It has been an unbelievable series of events."

"I can leave if you need some more alone time," he said theatrically reaching for the door handle but hoping she would ask him to stay.

"Oh, no. Please stay. There is no one I would rather be here with," she said moving toward him. She took him by the arm and let her hand drop down to his hand and led him over to a sofa and said, "Please sit with me."

Now, with the lights on, JP looked into her eyes and tried hard to decide on the most delicate way to tell her what was on his mind.

Anya, still holding his hand, said, "JP, you know I can read your thoughts. And to answer you and the General, yes, I am concerned about how Valerion will deal with the androids. There are thousands of Elonese in the convoy who deserve a chance to start a life on Sorrengia and I am concerned that Valerion may take that chance away from them if he is successful in controlling the robots."

JP's face was flushed when he realized that Anya might have gotten the impression that he had only been sent by the General to learn out about Valerion and the robots.

"Anya," JP said, "that is not the main reason I am here. Both the General and I sensed that something more than you said was bothering you about the situation on Sorrengia. General Walker's concern is how this might enhance Valerion's ability to cause us harm. My major concern is you and how I might help you deal with whatever is troubling you."

"You are so sweet to me, JP. I don't think you'll ever know how much your friendship has meant," said the little alien with a tear in her eye. "Unfortunately, the matter that you and General Walker noticed is between me and my father and others of my race. Quite simply, the problem is that I made a critical error in judgement when I sent Valerion to Sorrengia."

"How in Heaven's name could that be a critical problem?" asked JP, bewildered. "Everything that happened on Sorrengia was in the past."

Anya started to weep. She had never let anyone peer into her world, the world of the Builders. "Would you please just hold me, JP? I need you to hold me. No questions, please."

JP struggled trying to understand her dilemma but sensed that it was probably not something he could just figure out unless she opened up to him. He cradled her gently in his arms as she could no longer hold back her emotions. His heart ached.

As she gathered her feelings, she could hear the anguish in his mind. She looked up at JP and said, "Don't be troubled because you can't solve my problem. You are helping me more than you know just by being here with me."

JP, still holding her gently and looking down at her said, "I don't know how this works on your world but the feelings I have for you are a bit more than friendship."

She said, "Trust me, the feelings you are describing are the same in my world, in your world, and in thousands of worlds throughout the universe."

Just then, they both surrendered to their heart's impulses and their lips met.

Anya knew that opening herself to this man was expressly beyond the limits of acceptability for one of the Builders. However, the life of a Builder was often a lonely one and, at this time, the one thing in the universe she needed was to feel intimacy with someone who cared for her as much as she cared for him. The weight of the sadness and remorse in her heart was quickly being lifted by the force of this man's care and selfless devotion.

Knowing that she couldn't unring a bell that has already rung, the little Builder looked up and whispered quietly to JP, "Unless you have something else to do, I am going to turn out the lights so we can watch the stars."

"You must have been reading my mind," said JP.

"Why yes indeed I was," said Anya with an inviting love-smile.

The love-smile is like a secret code between two people who share the same deep feelings of intimacy for each other. It carries promises, wants, and desires and is both selfless and honest.

CHAPTER 25

It would be difficult to imagine a group of people more paranoid or afraid of each other than Valerion's inner circle from the former planet, Elon. As a result of this mixture of fear, bitterness, and megalomania, tension amongst each member of this group toward the others swirled to such extravagant heights that trust among them seemed nothing more than wishful thinking.

Valerion's power and influence as the President of the armada was being tested as never before. The main source of his control and peace of mind, was his army which was several thousand miles away on Sorrengia. The High Council was constantly in fear of being murdered by Valerion. Complicating the situation for the High Council was that they were under (the) increasing pressure from their constituents for answers about when they could occupy Sorrengia. The Council thoroughly distrusted Chancellor Nardin who increasingly stayed out of Valerion's way due to his coolness toward him.

It had been almost a week since Valerion had heard from Ludorn, the commander of his ground forces on the planet. Valerion ordered Zadorn to contact his brother and ask for a status update. Valerion wanted nothing more than to announce to the High Council that the conditions on their new home planet were under control. It made Valerion uneasy having his future well-being in the hands of someone else, even Ludorn.

Several hours later, Zadorn knocked on Valerion's door and told him that Ludorn had an update for him.

With Zadorn sitting across the stark, metal table from Valerion, communication was established and Ludorn appeared on the large view screen. Unable to wait for pleasantries, Valerion opened the conversation by saying, "Give me an update quickly. I need a little bit of good news."

"The natives are all dead. There is nothing more to be learned from them."

"As for the androids, they were all, at one time, living creatures whose bodies had received mechanical enhancements. Their new body parts, including computer memory chips in their heads, were powered by batteries which in turn were powered by strange crystals. We cannot find the source of the crystals and therefore we are unable to reenergize the robots with a compatible power source. We are attempting to use alternate sources of energy to power the mechanical units."

"What about the computer chips in their heads," asked Valerion. "What is the source of their programming?"

Ludorn replied, "We believe we have found the central computer but currently we cannot hack into it. What we do know, however, is that it is also powered by the same crystals as the robots."

Valerion barked at Ludorn, "I want every one of your people to be either looking for the source of the crystals or trying to come up with a power device that will energize the androids. There will be no time off for anyone until one of those two items is(are) located."

Without a response from Ludorn, Valerion ended the connection. "I need those androids to work," he snarled under his breath.

*****

The High Council requested a meeting with Valerion. Their constituents in the armada were getting increasingly impatient. The ongoing lack of information about the status of their arrival on their new home planet made the Elonese more agitated as each day passed. The requests for information caused Valerion's anxiety to soar to new heights each day as he had no information about the planet to pass on and, with his army gone, he had no way to shut them up.

Ludorn contacted his brother Zadorn and asked him to deliver a message to Valerion. "Tell Valerion that we have found a small supply of intact crystals. They were hidden away in one of their laboratories."

Valerion was on the view screen within minutes after hearing the news. "Tell me what you found, Ludorn."

"We have located enough of the crystals to power up three of the androids fully or perhaps partially power up about one dozen of them. We have been searching for days and these are all the crystals we have found."

"This is the best possible news. Let me know when the crystals have been installed but do not energize them until we can watch from Nightwind. This will be the day when we know that either the androids will be useful or we will have to build the New Elon with our own hands."

"Sir," said Ludorn, "It seems wise to power up one android and see what it can do before we use all the crystals in a demonstration."

Valerion scowled. He did not like having his orders questioned. "I believe that if we power up as many androids as possible and if they perform satisfactorily, then finding the crystals will be a minor distraction. It only makes sense that the crystals are nearby, probably in the mountains. Now, tell me when we can expect the demonstration."

"Tomorrow morning, sir," said Ludorn.

"Contact me when you are ready."

"As you wish," replied Ludorn.

Valerion turned to face his Chief of Security and said with his usual scowl, "Zadorn, contact Nardin and have him ready to attend the demonstration. If it is as successful as I believe it will be, I will need Nardin to contact the High Council so they can get back to their frantic constituents and give them some good news. These androids could be a huge help in getting our new society up and running by doing the heavy lifting."

"I will make those arrangements in person immediately," replied Zadorn.

*****

Both Zadorn and his brother, Ludorn, had always been ambitious after being raised in poverty. Zadorn and his brother Ludorn were raised in poverty, and this humble background made them hungry to succeed after joining the army. Their rise through the ranks attracted Valerion's attention. He was always on the lookout for eager young soldiers who would obey without question.

However, like the families of most soldiers, Zadorn and Ludorn's family had not been considered important enough to be included on the list of survivors in Valerion's armada. That their family had been left to die on Elon was a fact that gnawed constantly on the two brothers. Zadorn, the younger brother, could never shake the image of his mother and father burning to death in the front yard of their modest cottage.

Valerion had an extremely low regard for the soldiers individually. He considered them brutish, replaceable parts; useful idiots. Zadorn and Ludorn's positions were both high profile, isolated, and lonely. Neither dared share their innermost thoughts with anyone except each other. Despite the risk of exposure to Valerion, Zadorn contacted his brother on a secure, encrypted communication link. Or, at least, Zadorn believed it to be secure.

"Ludorn, are you ready for tomorrow's demonstration for Valerion?"

"We have barely had time to clean several of these machine beings and we have no idea which ones are working correctly. Honestly, no one knows how these androids will react when they are energized. The androids were always controlled by the main computer and it is powered by the same crystals that power the androids. Except for the few extra crystals we found for the four androids, there is no energy source for the computer."

Ludorn asked one final question, "What is the urgency for Valerion to hurry this process so quickly?"

"Valerion always relied on his army to provide him with protection. It is his source of power. The main thing that is driving him to make hasty decisions is that he feels great pressure to validate the idea that coming to this planet is a sound decision. Unfortunately for him, he has no one to back him up in case it is not. He knows the High Council hates him and would love to see him fail. But also, he knows that thousands of people in the armada are near the point of uprising if he cannot provide them with some reason for optimism."

Ludorn said, "I need to talk to Abraham Nardin. I worked under him once and he may still be an ally."

"Let me do it," said his younger brother.

"No. If this goes badly there is no need for both of us to go down instead of just one of us."

"Brother," said Zadorn with concern.

Ludorn interrupted him and said, "I am grateful to you, little brother. Just stay in the clear and do what Valerion expects. Watch your back and trust no one. We do not want to wind up dead at Valerion's hand like our parents."

"I think about them every day. Be careful, brother," said Zadorn who was again reminiscing about his dead parents.

*****

Once the communication between Ludorn and his brother ended, Ludorn collapsed into his chair and let his head fall back into the headrest with his eyes closed. Before he talked with Nardin, he needed to clear his head and consider his options. What he was thinking was treason by anyone's definition. In Valerion's world, people had disappeared for much, much less.

He thought to himself, "If the test of the robots goes well, Valerion will have saved face and will have provided a path for the creation of a new Elon for those on the convoy. If not, he will have failed spectacularly for the second time since leaving Elon. Such a fiasco would arguably provide enough blood in the water for any of his legion of critics to take him down. If the test with the robots fails, that will be the best time in years to exploit Valerion's vulnerability. But Nardin. What about Nardin? What will he do?"

*****

Nardin and Ludorn had known each other for many years due to their time in the military together.

Ludorn began the conversation by saying, "Tomorrow, at Valerion's insistence, we will energize several of the robots and see how or if they perform. Unfortunately, we have no way to control them because we have no access to the computer. He wants us to just turn them on and see what happens."

Nardin continued, "I plan to bring the entire High Council with me to the performance. It will not be easy to convince them to come with me but I think they need to see this first hand instead of hearing exaggerations or outright lies from Valerion. You know, Ludorn, he will blame you if the test goes badly. That is why we need the High Council there as witnesses posing as observers."

"You know that bringing the High Council to watch the demonstration runs contrary to Valerion's wishes. He wants as few observers as possible to avoid potential embarrassment in case the test goes badly."

"I will have to choose my words carefully if I want to convince him to allow them to attend. If I play to his arrogance that may overcome his fear of embarrassment."

"Zadorn will be inviting you formally in a few moments. Wait until then before contacting Valerion. My call to you is simply a heads-up and is strictly off the books. Understand?"

Nardin said, "as far as I am concerned, this conversation never happened."

Ludorn replied, "The moment you tell Valerion about bringing the High Council, he will be suspecting a trap. Unless you are very clever with your words, my friend, you will be marked as a traitor in his paranoid mind. Be very careful tonight. If I were you, I would be very hard to locate."

*****

"I believe I should have earned at least a speck of credibility with him for revealing the plot against him by the High Council. We will see how much that little bit of treachery was worth to him," thought Nardin as he approached the door to Valerion's chambers quite full of confidence.

"Mr. President, Zadorn tells me that tomorrow will be a big day for New Elon when we power up several androids and see how they perform. I know everyone in this armada will be relieved when they hear about their new home planet. Tomorrow's demonstration should satisfy everyone that you, with the assistance of the High Council, have not only saved the last of the Elonese people but also you have found a planet where we can all begin a new life. You will be hailed as gifted visionary," he said with his most deceitful smile.

"Nardin," Valerion said in almost a whisper as he stared down at the table, "I need those androids more than you can understand. I need them to be my new army. I need them to help me search the Universe and find Walker and his band of criminals. Walker must be destroyed."

"Surely, Mr. President, you know what a great victory it will be just to have our people on their new planet. Their new home."

"All I want is Walker's head on a stake. I can have no peace until I know he is dead."

"My Lord, let us not spend time on Walker. He may be half way across the Galaxy by now. I have no doubt he is running for his life. Let us celebrate our new home by watching the new planet unfold before us tomorrow as the High Council and I watch you reveal our new home. As you know, every single soul on this space convoy is desperate for information about the new planet."

"I am concerned about the High Council being here to witness the android demonstration. If it goes badly...."

Nardin interrupted Valerion and said, "Mr. President, not a soul on this armada cares one iota about the androids. Your people only want to start to start a new life and build their new home. Frankly, I am concerned about their self-control if they fail to get even a smattering of encouraging information about their new home. Tomorrow will be a perfect setting for you to showcase your vision in saving the Elonese from destruction."

"Alright, you can bring the whole band of scoundrels, if you must."

"If you remember, Mr. President, the last time we met with the High Council, I revealed an attempted coup against you. You might agree I saved your life. Surely you do not believe that my allegiance to you has wavered?"

Valerion was tiring of this back and forth with Nardin. He said, "If you must, be here with them shortly before 0900. I will hold you responsible for their behavior. Also, just so you are forewarned, they will all be searched by Zadorn personally. Understand?"

When Nardin left the room, Valerion turned to Zadorn and said, "It would not bother me if Nardin was to meet with an unfortunate accident tonight. Understand?"

"I do understand, Mr. President, but he saved your life the last time we met with the High Council. Are you certain you want him taken out at a time when, arguably, good friends are in short supply?"

"I don't need friends, Mr. Chief of Internal Security."

Zadorn could feel moisture in his armpits. His breath quickened. It was as if he was facing a poisonous snake coiled and ready to strike. "Not exactly, sir. I am trying to look out for your best interests in a very difficult time."

"You may be becoming a politician, Zadorn," he said but at the same time Valerion was thinking, "Is he telling me the truth or are he and Nardin working together to lull me into a false sense of security? I am not sure how much I can trust either of them now."

*****

After several hours of searching, Zadorn found Nardin in one of the passenger transports in a distant part of the convoy.

As he approached Nardin, he made a visual scan of his body for weapons. Nothing apparent. He thought to himself, "My life would be so much easier if I just shot him now. Valerion would be relieved but perhaps Ludorn and I might lose a valuable ally."

Before Zadorn could say a word, Nardin said, "I have spoken to all the High Council and most have agreed to be at Valerion's chambers before 0900. As much as they distrust me, they are all under tremendous pressure from their constituents for information."

Zadorn led the Chancellor around a corner in the hallway to a more private area where they could talk without being seen or overheard. Zadorn said, "I think you should know that I had to talk Valerion out of having you disappear tonight. He is beginning to question your support for him. If I were you, I would do whatever you can to change his mind."

"Why are you telling me this?"

"Maybe it is because my brother said that I might trust you. Or maybe Valerion told me to tell you this to keep you nervous."

"I'd like to think it was because I have known your brother for many years," said Nardin.

"Another reason I found you tonight is to tell you is that Valerion is absolutely obsessed with the idea of using the androids as his army. He is totally consumed with using those robots to find and destroy Walker. After that, I am certain he will turn his attention to ruling the Elonese in any way he sees fit. It will be grim."

"The game we are playing together is a deadly one, Zadorn. At this very moment he could be sending someone to kill you, me, or both of us. He is a psychopath of the highest magnitude and believes everyone is plotting to kill him."

"We need to think about what will happen after the demonstration. If it goes well, Valerion may wind up with an army of robots and have very little need for anyone else. If it goes badly, I cannot even imagine what his next move will be. Personally, I fear for my brother if the demonstration does not meet his expectations."

"I am afraid I cannot disagree with you. Valerion has a very low tolerance for failure."

"Except his own," replied Zadorn.

These two men could not be more different. Zadorn was an unemotional thug. His only attachment to any other living being was to his brother, Ludorn. Nardin, on the other hand, was the consummate politician. In Zadorn's mind, that meant he lied almost every time he opened his mouth.

The suspicion between the two men created a wall that neither could scale. Nardin stared into Zadorn's eyes searching for any hint of a shared understanding about a move against Valerion. He could detect nothing.

As with any conspiracy, someone must speak up first. However, both were frozen with fear that whatever they said would could reach Valerion and that alone would be enough to have them killed immediately.

Finally, frustrated, Zadorn broke the silence and said, "I must get back. Remember to tell those of the High Council that I will have to search each of them for weapons."

Nardin replied, "I hope the test of the androids is successful. If so, it should calm Valerion and give us all some breathing room. If it fails, I am afraid he will burst into an uncontrollable rage. That could be deadly for anyone nearby."

Zadorn said, "See you in a few hours." He then turned and walked away.

As Zadorn walked away from Nardin, both were disgusted with themselves for not having the courage to initiate a conversation about killing Valerion. They knew that the longer they kept company with Valerion, the higher was their chance of becoming a victim of one of his tirades. Despite fearing for their own lives, they both feared the president even more. Each, perhaps for different reasons, feared him so profoundly that they continued to live in dread of his reprisal.

****

After leaving Nardin, Zadorn returned to his small cabin for a few hours of rest before the demonstration began on Sorrengia. He put both of his weapons on the table in the middle of his room to clean them. He cleaned his weapons every night ensuring that they were in perfect working order. This time, however, he reached into a drawer and extracted a third weapon and cleaned it also. Some instinct whispered to him that he might need a second backup weapon. Such a thought was entirely out of character for this near robot of a soldier to whom repetition bred order and order led to comfort.

*****

At 0730, one and one-half hours before the scheduled time of the demonstration, Valerion summoned Zadorn to his chambers.

"I just called Nardin and told him that I have changed the location for the demonstration. I changed it to the observatory. The view screen will be in the observatory by 0800."

"That seems like a wise decision, Mr. President," said Zadorn. "One additional layer of security in the event of a surprise by any of your guests, am I correct?"

"You are learning, Zadorn."

They both smiled knowing smiles at each other but Zadorn was feeling ill inside. The idea that he was protecting this foul vermin's life was beginning to disgust him the longer he was around him. "It requires considerably more energy to do a task that you hate viscerally than to do one for which you have neutral or even positive feelings," he thought as their smiles melted away.

As they walked to the observatory, Valerion said, "I am more apprehensive about this gathering and the demonstration than usual. I have ordered Captain Dworat to meet me at the observatory along with six of the Palace Guard to add a further layer of security to the meeting."

"You know Dworat has a connection with Nardin," said Zadorn in a moment of reflexive obedience to his superior.

"I am aware of that but the Palace Guard is all I have left for security. Except for you, of course," replied Valerion. "By the way," Valerion said slowly as if he was carefully phrasing his next sentence, "how many side arms are you carrying now?"

Without hesitation, Zadorn snapped, "Two. My primary pistol and a backup."

As they turned the corner and approached the observatory, they could see Captain Dworat and the Palace Guard outside the entry to the airlock. Valerion slowed and turned to Zadorn, "Give me your two weapons. I told you that I was apprehensive about this meeting with people who have proven to be disloyal to me. I want to see to my own protection if the need arises."

"Sir," Zadorn asked as he was handing over his weapons, "my protection has always been sufficient. Why the change of heart?"

"Your protection is more than adequate except when I feel in such peril. Everyone in the meeting has reason to want to see me dead, including yourself. I have recently come to learn that you blame me for your parent's death on Elon. I would never have believed that affected you as much as it does if I not received copies of several transmissions between you and Ludorn. Most telling but not in a favorable way."

If Valerion knew about his conversations with Ludorn, perhaps he also knew about the conversation with Nardin. Zadorn surmised that his tenure as Chief of Internal Security was about to come to an end. In Zadorn's mind, this feeling was like seeing a sniper's kill shot coming toward you but knowing you could not get out of the way.

"My main concern this morning is with the androids. I need to see how they operate. I expect you to stand by my side, as usual, during the demonstration. We will talk about your future after it is over."

"Very well, Mr. President."

As Valerion and Zadorn approached the observatory, Captain Dworat's Palace Guard was waiting outside door number 1 of the airlock. The green light glared behind them.

As Zadorn looked at the Palace Guard, he wondered if one of the Palace Guards was being groomed by Valerion to take his place later this afternoon.

The airlock on this ship is a rectangular, airtight room with two air tight doors located about ten feet apart: The outer door (door number 1) opens to the inside of the ship. The other door, door number 2, opens into the pressurized observatory. It is called the inner door. Opening either door causes the opposite door to lock immediately, preventing a rapid depressurization of the entire ship. When both doors are closed, a green light is illuminated above both doors indicating that it is safe to open either of the doors. When one of the doors is open, a red light is illuminated and the opposite door is locked. In the instance of the observatory, the airlock prevents a rupture in the glass ceiling of the observatory, say from a meteor strike, from depressurizing the entire spaceship thus suffocating everyone on board.

Valerion said to Dworat, "Take your troops inside the observatory and do a safety sweep. If it is clear of weapons and explosives, send one of your troops to let me know and we will enter after you. After checking the observatory, you and your team, except for the two guarding the door number 2, will exit the airlock and scan the members of the High Council as they come to watch the demonstration. I expect the demonstration to last only a few minutes."

By 0830, the large view screen was set up on the oval conference table. None of the High Council had arrived. Zadorn, however, was trying to control his emotions which, for obvious reasons, were exploding inside him. He knew that no matter how the demonstration ended, he, his brother, and possibly Nardin were probably doomed.

This was it. Like a flash, a plan unfolded in Zadorn's head that was be the answer to his problems. The scheme was so simple it must be the only answer. He looked over his shoulder to assure himself that the green light in the airlock was on.

Zadorn faked a coughing attack. He doubled over as the cough became more intense while, at the same time, he reached into his tunic and felt for his second backup weapon, the one he concealed from Valerion. He slid his hand around the grip and armed it. He knew his next move had to be staged perfectly. He bolted up from his chair, turned and fired a shot into Valerion's midsection. It was not a lethal shot but a painful one. Next, he dashed for the door to the airlock, shooting the two unsuspecting members of the Palace Guard posted by the door per Valerion's orders.

As he reached the handle to the airlock, he turned and fired three shots into the glass ceiling of the observatory. Everyone in the observatory, except him, was in shock. Zadorn believed once he was inside the airlock, he was safe because everyone in the observatory would be gasping for breath and experiencing rapid decompression. They would be unconscious in fifteen seconds and dead about ninety seconds later.

As soon as Zadorn exploded the glass dome he felt the pressurized air being pulled instantly out of the observatory into the vacuum of space. Next, he pushed down on the handle to unlock the door to the airlock but found it locked. He looked up and found himself staring into the red light. "Oh God, how could this happen?" He looked at the window to the door and saw Nardin outside the air lock holding door number 1 open. Nardin was preventing him from escaping to the safety of the pressurized space ship. His plan had failed, his heart was pounding from lack of oxygen, and he was going to die with Valerion.

Nardin arrived late because he was trying to summon the nerve to kill Valerion as soon as he entered the observatory. Instead, he witnessed Zadorn's entire dramatic episode which took less than five seconds. Nardin was holding the outer door open while he decided whether to save Zadorn or not.

Nardin looked through the window to the observatory. Zadorn was already starting to weaken from lack of oxygen and was mouthing the words, "Help me." Valerion was trying to rise from the chair where he was shot while holding his midsection which was gushing blood. Nardin stepped into the airlock and closed the door behind him. This unlocked the door to the observatory. Nardin opened door number 2 and pulled Zadorn inside the airlock. When Nardin opened the door to the observatory all the air in the airlock was sucked into the observatory and then into space leaving Nardin and Zadorn in as bad a situation as those in the observatory. Zadorn looked out the window at door number 2. Valerion was reaching for the door handle but Zadorn closed the door to the observatory with a mighty pull, jerking the handle out of Valerion's bloody grasp.

Quickly, Nardin reopened door number 1 which locked door 2. Nardin and Zadorn had escaped with their lives but Valerion did not.

Valerion saw Zadorn deny him entry into the airlock which sealed his fate as retribution for Valerion having killed Zadorn's parents. It was an empty victory for Zadorn but one that brought him some vindication.

Barely able to believe their good fortune, Nardin and Zadorn rushed to the air lock window to look for Valerion. With his last bit of strength, he was trying desperately to open the door. Instead of opening the door, he looked up at the window and saw Zadorn and Nardin looking curiously into his face while he took his last few gasps. Oh, how he hated them but not for long. Within seconds, all that was left of Valerion was a bloody handprint on the door handle to the air lock. The airlock had done its job.

Nardin and Zadorn quickly turned their heads to look for the Palace Guard but they were down the hall greeting members of the High Council who were exiting the elevator. Zadorn was safe from incrimination.

Zadorn said, "If you count those like my parents who he could have saved but didn't feel like it was worth his time, the number of people on Elon that he killed is in the millions. I don't feel like a hero for what I did but there is little doubt that the Universe is better off without him."

Nardin said, "Let's contact your brother and tell him what happened. I don't think we need the demonstration today or probably ever."

Zadorn said, "I don't know how to thank you for opening that door. I probably didn't deserve to be spared but I am glad you did it. Thank you."

"I know Valerion told you to take me out but, for some reason, you talked him out of it. That took nerve and I am grateful to you for sparing my life last night. I guess we are even. I think the story we need to tell about this morning is that Valerion died from a rupture in the observatory and the rapid decompression thereafter. Okay with you?"

"Oh, yea. That's just how I saw it."

In the ensuing hours, Nardin and Zadorn met with the High Council to announce Valerion's death and that Nardin would take over as interim president until an election could be held within 60 days. The mood in the High Council was one of elation and a general air of contentment and optimism pervaded both the High Council and the rest of the armada. Nothing remained of Valerion except a legacy of death and favoritism.

Anya and her father shared vicariously in the joy of the occasion. Neither of them took any credit for Zadorn's miraculous plan but neither of them denied it either.

Valerion's death was an opportunity for a new beginning for the remnants of the Elonese people. Now the Builders were now able to complete their task of assisting the Elonese build a new future without fear of being ruled by a treacherous despot.

CHAPTER 26

With JP trying to sift through the confusing details of Anya's description of the demise of the Sorrengian people, Walker set out to have a face to face with Megan. "Exactly, what was it that prompted her to release the five thugs out of their cells?" His misgivings about her ultimate loyalty reared its ugly head as he couldn't imagine a single reason for setting those thugs loose.

Looking for Megan, Walker went to the bridge to see how long before the ship reached the Naroobian system for a reunion with his brother and The People. "We are on the course given to us by Anya," said Samantha. "With any luck we should be there in thirty-six hours."

"By the way," said Walker. "Have you any idea where Megan is?"

Samantha answered, "She told me that she was going to the nursery to visit the youngsters. She said that she had gotten quite fond of one of them."

"Very nice," he said with a smile but somehow her being fond of little children and her letting a group of would-be killers who tried to commandeer the ship just did not add up in his mind. He was worried about her true intentions again.

Megan spotted him as soon as he stepped out of the shiny steel elevator. She waved to him, got up, and walked toward him.

As she was walking toward him, she said, "there is something I have to tell you that's been bothering me."

Before she could start her second sentence, Walker said in an emotionless voice, "What you better come up with is a good reason why you let those wastes of skin lose to put so many lives in danger."

Megan hung her head in remorse and said, "You had no way of knowing this but the four men that you dragged down to their cells were part of a five-man gang. I had no intention of releasing these jerks from their cells but while I was talking to them, the fifth man came up behind me and knocked me out. He took my sidearm and my keys. I was unconscious when they let themselves lose."

"Okay, Megan, but why go down there to confront them at all," Walker asked. "What did you have to gain by that?"

She said, "Because I knew what they were capable of, I thought I would question them to see what their intentions were. I felt a sense of safety as they were behind bars. Yes, I know, that was not the best idea of all time but I was feeling a strong allegiance to your crew and shipmates. It felt like a risk I had to take and I felt safe with them behind bars. I am sorry."

Megan buried her head in her hands when she thought of the possible ramifications of her misguided mistake.

Walker said, "The Yardak were bad but the thought of all that we have risked going up in smoke and being returned to Valerion makes me question your...." He was interrupted in mid-sentence by an urgent call from JP.

"General, I have it on very good authority that Valerion is dead. He was killed by an accident in the observatory this morning, "JP said very excitedly.

"Is this some kind of joke, JP?" Walker questioned.

"No, sir. Anya's father was monitoring the thought waves from Valerion's armada and, as you can imagine, that is all the people in his armada can talk about. The number two man in charge, Chancellor Nardin, is assuming command until elections can be held. No one is grieving over the loss of Valerion. In fact, the entire population was relatively giddy upon hearing the news."

"My God," thought Walker. "Now all those people on Valeion's transports have a chance at a decent life. My guess is that reenergizing the cyborgs may not be on anyone's list of priorities."

"What was the message from JP?" asked Megan.

"The message was that Valerion is dead. The pall that has been held over everyone on Elon, even including The People, has been lifted."

Walker felt certain that the news of Valerion's "death" would be of great interest to everyone on the former Prison Ship. JP suggested to Walker,

"Why not ask Samantha if she would do the honors of making the announcement." She was elated at the opportunity to address her shipmates and give them the good news.

JP turned to Walker and said, "General, since we left Elon, we have been going non-stop from one crisis to another. I think it is time to relax before we get to Lordune."

"My friend, I don't know if I am able to relax anymore," the General said with a smile. "I feel like we need to meet with Eli and find out what we are getting ourselves into on Lordune. I really hate to say it but it all sounds almost too good to be true. Please find Anya and bring her to the bridge and we will have a chat with Eli." After that, JP and the General went their separate ways.

Within minutes, the elevator door opened to the bridge. JP and Anya stepped out onto the shiny floor. Samantha greeted them as they were now on her turf. The General who arrived several minutes earlier, walked over to Anya and greeted her warmly, saying, "We are in need of a chat with you and Eli. JP and I were wondering if you two could brief us as to the conditions on Lordune. I am certain that The People are anxious to hear what their new planet will be like."

"My father and I are both aware of your concerns regarding Lordune," Anya said, "and we believe we can set your mind at ease with a brief video-chat. Let's move into the briefing room at the far side of the bridge."

The General turned and called to the captain, "Samantha, I believe you should join us.

"Yes, sir," she replied with a wide smile.

Eli opened the discussion as follows: "As a bit of background, we are members of a group of intergalactic travelers called The Builders, and we are based in the Naroobian system. Our sole purpose is to assist developing civilizations to become self-sufficient and to develop their capabilities so they can not only thrive but also be able to assist others who are struggling. Another one of our functions is to help those in need of assistance, such as the people of Elon, to escape from civilization ending situations."

"But Eli," Walker said, "why do you do these things for people you don't even know. You treat us like family which we clearly are not."

"Seth, while it may appear obvious to you that we are not family because we do not look alike, to us it is clearly obvious that we are family. We are all children of the Creator of the Universe and we are instructed to go forth and bring loving assistance to those in need."

"It may make it easier for you to understand if I tell you that we are interplanetary missionaries. We do things in the universe that no one else could or would do. Who else in the universe would or could provide the assistance we did for you when you were escaping from Valerion?" Eli continued: "Obviously you were desperately in need of a new home planet after escaping from Elon and we believe that Lordune will be more than acceptable. We anticipate that you will be landing on Lordune, which, as you already know, has a cloaking system that hides your new home's existence from anyone who does not have the uncloaking technology."

"We are humbled," said Walker. "This clears up a lot of things. However, let me bring up some more mundane matters. What is the planet surface like and are there others on the planet with us?"

Eli said, "I knew this question would come up. The planet is rich in natural resources and it has wonderful land for growing crops. You will be located near a village of native Naroobians. I believe you and your people can be of great assistance to the Naroobians and they will be able to help you adjust to the new home."

The question-and-answer session went on for several hours until everyone was exhausted.

Eli ended the session with the following statement, "General, you should be on the ground within 24 hours and your brother will be joining you shortly thereafter. I can't tell you what a pleasure it has been to assist you and The People because you have shown yourselves to be a truly honorable and capable. Once you are situated on the ground, I would like to discuss some plans I have that could involve you and some of your crew."

"I look forward to it, Eli," replied Walker.

*****

The first individual to greet Walker's ship when it landed on Lordune was Eli. As Walker exited the massive space cruiser, he saw someone who he surmised to be Eli because he was at the bottom of the gangplank and the crowd of interested spectators gave the lone individual space as would be befitting someone of high importance. Walker struggled to keep his expectations and fears to himself lest Eli read his mind and be forewarned concerning Walker's state of mind.

When Walker reached the bottom of the gangplank, his eyes met those of the lone individual at the bottom of his descent. "May I know your name," asked Walker.

"As you may have surmised, I am Eli," said the one-man reception committee. "I am ever so delighted to welcome you here to my family's home planet of Lordune. We have so much to learn from each other and, God willing, I believe that before long we will be one big, happy family."

Walker bowed his head in respect and thanked his host profusely, "for guiding us to what appears to be an even better resolution to, or escape from, Elon than I could have ever imagined."

"Seth, one of the annoying characteristics of our race is our ability to read minds, as you have experienced during your trip to Lordune. As far as mind reading is concerned, I understand that you are having trust issues with Megan. If I may be so bold, let me assure you that Megan did not betray your trust when the hooligans broke out of confinement and threatened the ship. That was purely an accident for which she is truly sorry. Let me leave it at this but I believe that you might want to give her the benefit of the doubt and see what happens. That, my friend, is the end of my meddling."

"I must tell you, Eli, that is one big, thorny problem and I am grateful for the 'insight'".

"Before I let you loose to reunite with what appears to be five or six thousand of your closest friends, The People, let me propose one additional challenge," Eli said. "You have no way of knowing the facts concerning what I am about to say, but your having fled from Elon and being forced to find a new planet to call home is not unique in space. The universe is so vast and the number of habitable planets is so incalculable that it should not come as a surprise that there are numerous groups of beings, like yourselves, who are either wandering the universe in search of a viable home planet or just beginning to start the process of searching for a new place to call home. Having gotten to know you during your treck for survival, I would like to explore the possibility of you and some of your crew joining The Builders as we offer safety and survival to others in the universe who find themselves in desperate need of our services."

"That is really an amazing prospect, Eli, but my first reaction to your proposal is that you and Anya were able to help us so unbelievably is due to some of your amazing gifts: gifts that we do not even come close to having."

"Let me assure you, Seth, you haven't seen half of our special talents," said Eli with a wide grin.

Seth's head was spinning at the possibilities. He said to Eli, "Am I to assume that there would have to be some modifications to our existing capabilities should we join your group of space angels?"

"Yes, indeed, General. We don't send anyone into space unless he or she is fully equipped to handle the tasks required. Think it over. You have natural leadership skills and abilities that most will never develop. These are skills that The Builders need."

"Good God, this is unbelievable," said Walker slowly and thoughtfully.

"Yes, Seth, my friend, God is good and, with Him, you will find that the unbelievable becomes possible."

www.ingramcontent.com/pod-product-compliance
Lightning Source LLC
Chambersburg PA
CBHW020613250626
47154CB00004B/1487